The End of My Career

The End of My Career

The sequel to
My Brilliant Career

MILES FRANKLIN

With a Foreword by Verna Coleman

ST. MARTIN'S PRESS • NEW YORK

Copyright © 1981 by Miles Franklin Estate
For information, write: St. Martin's Press,
175 Fifth Avenue, New York, N.Y. 10010
Manufactured in the United States of America

10 9 8 7 6 5 4 3 2 1
First Edition

Library of Congress Cataloging in Publication Data

Franklin, Miles, 1879-1954.
    The end of my career.

        Previously published as: My career goes bung. 1946.
        Sequel to: My brilliant career.
        I. Title.
PR9619.3.F68M9 1981   823   81-8772
ISBN 0-312-25075-4   AACR2

FOREWORD

Bursting with youthful energy out of the confines of life in a dreary, drudging farming community Stella Maria Sarah Miles Franklin wrote *My Brilliant Career* between September 1898 and November 1899. It was published in 1901 when she was twenty-one. Based largely on her own, more bitter than sweet, adolescent experience it purported to be the "autobiography" of sixteen-year-old Sybylla Melvyn who shocked the narrow-minded bush community of 'Possum Gully with her mildly outrageous behaviour and advanced views, particularly on the position of women.

In 1902 little firebrand Miles completed a sequel, *The End of My Career*, which carried Sybylla's adventures a little further. As a successful author the high-spirited Sybylla — in meek attire of white muslin dress and cashmere stockings, and with her hair still down her back in schoolgirl fashion —, descended on fashionable Sydney, and was taken up as an infant prodigy by the social literary elite. This novel was not published until forty years later when it appeared (in 1946) as *My Career Goes Bung*. Basically this was the original manuscript, for Miles Franklin wrote in her preface: "I have kept faith with that girl who once was I. I have not meddled by corrections."

After the small furore created by *My Brilliant Career* everyone had expected that the fresh and startling author would produce another success quickly. What happened? Why was the second work so long in reaching publication?

1

In her 1946 preface Miles Franklin remarked that the novel had been regarded as too audacious for publication. Publisher George Robertson had returned the manuscript in November 1902 saying: "It isn't feasible ... you've made me jolly glad I didn't meet you ... not even 200% would induce me to publish." Sybylla-Miles, the pet of Sydney society, had turned out to be a little wild-cat and had given the social set of the day a mild clawing. Certainly Robertson had recognized Rose Scott, *grande dame* of the city's only salon, in one of the characters. Further, Australia's "one great literary man", calculating, ruthless but magnetic Goring Hardy, might have been taken to represent "Banjo" Paterson with whom Miles Franklin had been entangled in a literary-emotional relationship during 1902. The spectre of libel actions loomed too large and Robertson at that time had no choice but to refuse publication.

However the audacity of the work went much deeper than the scratching satire of social pretensions. *My Career Goes Bung* was emphatically feminist. Sybylla was concerned to fight her way through the undergrowth of established customs and codes, to beat out a path to a position of independence and freedom. Her attitudes, accepted and fashionable as they are today, were jolting to the complacencies of eighty years ago. She was an early feminist heroine well ahead of her time, an angry young woman and often an unhappy one.

She was angry about the general standing of women, that they had been classed with idiots and children in suffrage matters. She was deeply dismayed at the prison marriage seemed to build and at the unhappiness of many bush women in their maternal role — "broken-down drudges talking of uterine problems and the weariness of child bearing". And she was disgusted by the gulf between tinselly notions of romantic love and the grossness of much sexual reality. The attentions of unattractive men, old Mr. Grayling, fat Gaddy and clumsy Henry Beauchamp were repellent. So though she had a sharp understanding of the cold-hearted selfishness of Goring Hardy she welcomed the elements of glamour and excitement in her flirtation with such a handsome literary lion.

This determined independence of spirit, lack of cant and naive straightforwardness about sex were too harshly honest for the sentimental conventions of the close of the Victorian era. Rebellious Sybylla-Miles rejected in too blunt a manner the role set out for women. "You don't allow a woman any standing except by being the annexation of a man." she said to Henry Beauchamp. Eighty years later that is still a familiar cry.

From her meagre twenty-two years experience in a strait-laced society Miles Franklin was attempting in 1902 to deal with a new question in fiction, or perhaps more frankly with an old one. Who shall rule in the war between the sexes? Or can a sexual relationship be a true partnership with both man and woman living fully and happily? Or is that in the nature of things impossible? Twenty years later D. H. Lawrence was to be thought outrageous when he carried the analysis of the power struggle between men and women in their sexual relationships much further and deeper.

Today *My Career Goes Bung* still has something to say in this arena, though to modern taste it may seem somewhat too intense in tone and preaching in manner. However the book is also a romp, a gentle satire softened by the author's laughter at the antics of fellow players in a difficult game. And the courage and honesty of Sybylla are warming — a difficult girl perhaps, but it was a difficult world. Sharply through the youthful comedy the typical note of Miles Franklin sounds, defiant, uncompromising. "I rebel with all my living force against sitting down under life as it is," declares Sybylla — Stella Miles Franklin throughout her long life of struggle certainly never sat down.

VERNA COLEMAN
1980

TO ALL YOUNG AUSTRALIAN WRITERS
GREETINGS!

Precocious effort in art is naturally imitative, but in localities remote from literary activity there is no one for the embryo writer to copy. Thus I was twelve before I wrote anything to draw attention to myself. I must have been nearly thirteen when the idea of writing novels flowered into romances which adhered to the design of the trashy novelettes reprinted in the *Supplement to the Goulburn Evening Penny Post*. These stories, secretly devoured, presented a world enchanting to budding adolescence. They were prinked with castles with ivied towers and hooting owls, which were inhabited by the unaccommodating guardians, thrilling seducers and more thrilling rescuers of titled maidens, as pure as angels. I used to read my versions to two or three girls, who still gaily recall the entertainment we thus manufactured for ourselves.

An Englishman, to whom some of these lucubrations were shown, directed me to the Australian scene as the natural setting for my literary efforts. The idea sprouted. Huh! I'd show just how ridiculous the life around me would be as story material, and began in sardonically humorous mood on a full-fledged novel with the jibing title *My Brilliant (?) Career*. I remember declaring my need of a striking name for the rampageous heroine of my ambition. An elder friend—beloved by her young neighbours for her sympathy — thereupon

5

gave me her two Christian names Penelope and Sybylla, which she said were wasting, as she was known by a diminutive — Penny. This was an inspiring gift.

But INEXPERIENCE cannot possibly achieve any intended artistic effect. Removed as I was from anyone equipped to understand or direct my literary attempts it was inevitable that I, of all my audience, should be the most flabbergasted. The literalness with which *My Brilliant Career* was taken was a shock to one of any imagination.

My Career Goes Bung was planned as a corrective. I discussed with my father the absurdity of girls from all over the continent writing to tell me that I had expressed their innermost lives and emotions — confidences of fellowship in introversion, whereas I was a healthy extrovert. My father, equally with myself, lacked knowledge of practising authors, or association with people who had any conception of what authorship of fiction might entail. But he had wisdom.

"You mustn't spoil what you have done," he said. "You see, you have created an imaginary reality, and you must stick to it now. Something would be hurt in all those discontented little girls if they felt that your story lacked foundation. Besides, they are many, and I and you are only two."

I felt that my father did not quite understand, and so did not show him the story. Now I know that he was a spiritual genius in a community where there was no realisation of his giftedness nor any more employment for it than for a Spanish comb in a bald head.

The pother raised by Sybylla Penelope in print so petrified me that I closed her book and have not yet reopened it. Could I bring myself to re-read it I could, perhaps,

6

fabricate an essay to air the dubious guesses of psycho-analysis: but that would be a preface to my first printed volume while this is a foreword to its aftermath.

This was deposited in a portmanteau of MSS and finally left with someone in Chicago, U.S.A. while I went to the World War, which is now seen to have been merely practice manoeuvres for Global Armageddons. When I returned this caretaker said Mr. X had needed a bag, and, as my old grip was quite out of fashion and contained nothing but useless papers, she had known I would be glad to oblige him. I was assured Mr. X had put all the papers in the furnace: I need have no fear that they had been left about. I made no complaint, being as sure as the caretaker that my MSS were of no consequence. Nevertheless I regret the loss of stories and plays, which glowed at the time, and which will not come again. I thought *My Career Goes Bung* had gone with this collection, and had forgotten the copy of it which survived in an old trunk valiantly preserved all the years by my mother.

I opened the packet with trepidation and to my relief found entertainment, but that, as Sybylla Penelope Melvyn would say, may be due solely to egotism. The MS had a dedication of gratitude to someone indicated by initials, but I cannot recall who this was nor why I should have been grateful to him or her. There was also a preface by Peter McSwat, "Who kept a diary and paid his debts." Time has cancelled this topical illusion, and it has been deleted with some matter which has been disposed of elsewhere. Otherwise I have kept faith with that girl who once was I. I have not meddled by corrections which would have resulted, probably, in no better than the substitution of one set of solecisms and clichés by another, for such abound in even the greatest English novels.

The novel returned to me out of the past with the impact of a discovery. Though a work of fiction, the people in it are oddly familiar: their story has with time shed any character but that of reality. It is now an irrefutable period piece, and, in the light of EXPERIENCE, it is to be discerned that while intentionally quite as little, unintentionally it was equally as autobiographical as my first printed romance; no more, no less.

This second portrait of Sybylla Penelope was classified as delicious by the only person to whom it was submitted at the time: that it was also regarded by him as "too audacious for publication" seems quaint today, and indicates how smug behaviour must have been when it was written. It is to-day inveterately dedicated to all Australian writers who were as young, who are as young, and who each decade for ever will be forthcoming as young as I was when first I foolhardily tried to write.

MILES FRANKLIN,
AUSTRALIA.

This tale's as true as true can be,
   For what is truth or lies?
So often much that's told by me
   When seen through other eyes,
Becomes thereby unlike so much
   These others tell to you,
And if things be the same as such,
   What is a scribe to do?

Why, tell his tale of course, my friend,
   Or hold his tongue for aye,
Or wait till fictive matters mend,
   Which may be by-and-bye.
So here's a tale of things a-near
   That you may read and lend
Without a fear — you'll need no tear—
   It hasn't any end.

Chapter One.

Explanatory.

A wallaby would have done just as well as a human being to endure the nothingness of existence as it has been known to me. This, I suppose, is why I want to tell of the only two lively things that have happened in a dull, uninteresting life. You don't know me from a basket of gooseberries, or wouldn't if only I had kept myself to myself, but as I didn't, I shall endure the embarrassment of bringing myself to your attention again in an explanatory postscript. In company with ninety-nine per cent. of my fellows, the subject of self is full of fascination to me. There are cogent reasons for this.

One of the interesting happenings is my entanglement with Henry Beauchamp. The other is my experience in writing a new style of autobiography. Such a departure grew out of my satiation with the orthodox style. I shall deal with the autobiography first. These notes are slightly and somewhat expurgatedly compiled from my diary.

I was at that stage of chrysalism when boys dream of becoming bushrangers, engine drivers, or champion pugilists. Nothing so garishly simple relieves a girl. I yearned to make the whole world into a beautiful place where there would be no sick and starving babies, where people of advancing years could be safe from penury, where all the animals could be fat and happy, and even our little sisters, the flowers, might not be bruised or plucked against their wish. The prospect of settling down to act tame hen in a tin pot circle, and to acknowledge men as superior merely owing to the accident of gender, revolted me.

Life among boys and girls at an institution such as the Stringybark Hill Public School, ere adolescence has arrived to mess things up, is a good example of democracy. There were no wealthy within competitive reach, money did not count to any extent, and beauty and birth did not count at all. We never heard of such things. Only the merit of brains and honesty weighed in the school room, and athletic prowess coupled with fair play on the playground.

Any sort of lessons except long addition sums were a joy and sinecure to me. On the playground, though small, I was fleet of foot and exceptionally agile, could vault as high as any boy of my own age till I was twelve, and was always chosen as captain whether the game happened to be cricket, rounders or prisoners' bar. A balance was preserved in my status by the fact that the dunces at lessons were always the best bats or runners outside, and that athletes when grown up had so much more glory than mere scholars.

I was impatient to be done with school so that I could take hold of life in the big world. I could not understand why people stayed in some lone hole with no more spunk in them than a milch cow, while the universe elsewhere teemed with adventure.

I expected to continue in enjoyment of the friendship and affection of my fellows, working for and winning a high place in all the activities that I essayed. I thought that there would be any number of activities to choose from. I was sure of winning love and acclamation because I never cheated in a game or put on airs over my ascend-

12

ancy in them, and eagerly shared anything and everything within my power.

Thus came the last day under the rule of the gentle old teacher in the little slab school house among the tall trees on the stringy bark range. Old Harris, as we called him behind his back, got drunk on occasion but was condoned by the kindly settlers because he knew and loved each child individually. He could bring what there was out of the thickest skulls and I riated unrebuked and highly encouraged within his jurisdiction. He had been educated at one of the great colleges in England. I don't know which as he never mentioned it to the simple circle of Stringybark Hill. He was supposed to be related to big swells but that likewise he never mentioned unless he was a bit tipply and some flash intruder was putting on airs. He had the manners of an angel, a dear kind face, and wouldn't have harmed a grasshopper. These qualifications earned him the protection of the rudest and crudest. He taught a mere handful of children the rudiments of education for less than £3 a week and boarded with a family who were industrious, honest and kind, but could offer him no congeniality of mind or companionship of knowledge.

Ma condemned his fecklessness to be stuck there, but Pa would rub the top of his head — his own head — and remark, "At Old Harris's age life boils down to a decent bed and a good feed, and those things are his."

At the end of my last day with him he patted me on the shoulder—an unusual liberty for this diffident soul. He never seemed to have any egotism except when he was drunk. It must have been ingrowing like squeezed toenails. He made a little speech over me, the kind which youth accepts as drivel at the time, but which comes back vividly when youth has grown towards this drivelling

13

knowledge itself. It returns to me now in the drivellage of my twentieth year, and here it is.

"Sybylla, you are a good girl—clean and true—and a gifted one to boot. You are as game as a young lion but I fear that the opposing forces will break your heart. You are a glad young thing now, but with your ability and temperament, alas, it will take more than ordinary conditions to keep you happy. You have a quicker brain than any scholar I ever had, but that will not help you unless you use it to hide the fact of its existence and to enhance your beauty; and of beauty you have ample to secure what would satisfy most of your sex, but which will never content you, so I might as well hold my tongue. At any rate, good fortune attend you. The old school house will be dull and lonely without you."

I thought that he must have had a drop, but now when he is dead and six years have passed, I simply know that his experience of life was more than mine.

I was let out in advance and he stood looking after me as I swung down the path between the young trees which I had helped to plant on by-gone Arbor Days. Affection is a terribly binding thing. It always keeps me from breaking bonds, so I turned back every few steps to wave to the old man with a wistful regret that he was a finished chapter and that I could not take him with me into the glamorous young world towards which I was headed.

I had two miles to go by a short cut, which I followed for the joy of fallen logs to vault, and I sprang high every yard or two for the gum leaves that splashed their outline on the ground. The sky was a washing-bag blue with mountainous white clouds of thunderous splendour piled in the west. What a sunset it would be! I revelled in every scrap of beauty that came my way, and was excited

14

to picture the beauty and adventure that I was going to broach beyond the ragged horizon to be seen from the tall fence post. The loveliest most thrilling thing in sight was the road that led from the front paddock to Goulburn, then on and on to Sydney—first port of call in my voyage of conquest. I climbed on to the garden post for a view before entering the house, my school days past.

"What are you doing there like a tom-boy?" inquired Ma. "You must change your ways now. The happiest days you'll ever know are over—all play and no work and worry. You'll find life a different matter."

LIFE a different matter—I should hope so!—like a blue ocean of adventure calling with a deafening invitation to embark.

CHAPTER TWO.

THE FETTERED ROUND.

But how to get on to that ocean? I was on a small weedy waterhole that seldom swelled into a stream and there were many snags. Upon leaving school these multiplied like fury.

I entered into the life of struggling incompetent selectors. The chief burden of that, for the women, was unrestricted child-bearing, and I was now a woman, as Ma reminded me, a fact which made me rebellious. Ma said I was always a wilful and contradictory imp and that during the throes of rearing me, she was frequently put to such confusion that despite I was her first and last and only child there were times when she could have cheerfully wrung my neck. Ma said most girls felt the way I did at first, but soon settled down. All girls wished that they were men.

At that I flashed out like a tornado, insulted. Never in my life had I a wish to be a man. Such a suggestion fills me with revulsion. What I raged against were the artificial restrictions.

Girls! I do not address those feeble nauseating creepers who seem to fit into every one of the old ruts, the slimy hypocrites who are held up as womanly, but those who have some dash and spirit. You remember what we had to learn, girls, things that one cannot write in plain print or else truth would be abused as indecency; and there were other things too subtle to be expressed even to the elect,

16

but which wielded the strongest subjecting influence. The dead dank gloom that settled on us upon learning that the eternal feminine was the infernal feminine! But Ma always said, "You'll have to get used to it. There is no sense in acting like one possessed of a devil."

A man can get used to having his legs cut off, and women have even greater endurance, or, seeing the conditions under which they live and work and dress and reproduce their species, they would have been extinct with the Great Auk, and what a pity they weren't!

Girls! Do you remember how we loathed the correct meek merely sexy specimens who had none of our foolhardy honesty, or any unsmutched ideals of life and love? We clamoured for the opportunity to be taken on our merits by LIFE: we wanted to play it as we played our games, where, if there was any doubt about us being bowled out, we did not want to hold on, we laid down our bats without whimpering.

The first foul blast from the tree of knowledge was that we weren't to be allowed any unadulterated HUMAN merits. Sexual attractions alias WOMANLINESS was to be our stock-in-trade. If we did not avail ourselves of it we were defenceless, and might even be execrated. How we abhorred the cunning girls who found no trouble with their role. In school they had been ranked by attainment, and their marks had seldom risen even to FAIR. Now in the hierarchy of mere gender their pandering intelligence was to score every time. We could come into line or find ourselves on an outside track alone.

Girls, how did you take it?

It seemed to develop into a storm between Ma and me. Ma at last said, "Bother it, I have nothing to do with it. It is God's will."

It was a relief to be indignant with God, but a trial not to be able to get at Him in any way. In my perturbation I collided with Great-aunt Jane, who said that the Lord loveth those whom He chasteneth. His way of saving the world did not appear to me as efficient for a being who was all-powerful. He so loved the world that He gave His only begotten Son to save it, and allowed Him to be nailed on a cross in ghastly agony — without saving anything considerable as far as history shows.

"Heaven knows what He would have permitted to be done to a daughter," I remarked.

Aunt Jane stood this pretty well. "Ah," she laughed, "You'll grow to sense. A husband and children of your own will put you in your place."

The dire soul-crushings with which old wives threaten me consequent upon the glories of motherhood are enough to quell a quadruped. Aunt Jane repudiated the blame too, and said I should have to wait until the next world to have things righted.

"According to what I have heard, a woman who has had the hell of bearing twelve children to give some male object a heaven of begetting is just as likely to go to hell as the father: and the next world's joys are open equally to men, more so, in fact. That next-world-payment-of-debts is sloppy rubbish," I snorted.

"You have a great deal to learn," said Auntie. "You are a rude ignorant girl. If you persist in thinking as you do, you'll come to harm."

Pa rubbed his hair up on end and gently remarked, "What is coming to harm in this debate, Aunt Jane, is your theology."

Pa's words fell as healingly as rain on the dust. I was

18

sorry I had been rude to Auntie. When I got Pa alone I questioned him further, and he said, as if talking to himself, "As high as a people rises, so high will be its gods."

"The trouble with the Church of England God," Pa continued, "is that he is made in the image of some darned old cackling prelate, so mean and cowardly that the Devil, for consistency and ability, is a gentleman beside him." Pa had a twinkle in his eye as he added, "But you know, it isn't gentlemanly to upset people of less mental powers than yourself; besides, it is dangerous. Think as much as you like, my girl, but let sleeping dogs lie unless you can do some real good by waking them up."

Great-aunt spends a lot of time with us. She says Pa is the nicest man she has ever known in a house, that I should thank God on my knees every night for such a parent. This so differs from Ma's inculcations that I would attribute it to Auntie's love of contradiction, only that under cross-questioning she says that had she had such a father when a girl she would have thought herself in heaven. Her father was an unmerciful autocrat. His daughters had to live their lives under cover, so to speak, like mice. I wish I could be so dominating, but judging by Grandma and Ma and myself, this progenitor's progenitiveness is becoming diluted with the generations.

I concede that technically Ma is my primary parent and Pa merely secondary. The question of woman's emancipation and the justice which is her due make this fatally clear in theory, but when it comes to the practice of an affection which springs spontaneously from my human breast, Pa can have no second place; and when it comes to being understood, well—but—but—Ma says having children of my own will teach me. I wonder what.

I had lots of other stuffing in me too. Resiliently I renewed my attack on LIFE. Rebellion against artificial WOMANLINESS did not interfere with all that rushed out of my mind on the wings of imagination. There was one great recreation open to me, even at 'Possum Gully, which was a sop to energy. I could ride. I could ride tremendously. I loved horses and seemed to become part of them. In the district were any number of good horses, most of them owned by bachelors. As one of these bachelors said, "A lovely high-spirited girl is just the thing to top-off a good horse."

All kinds of horses, from racing stallions to hunting mares, were brought to me with the owners included as escorts and the source of chocolates in wonderful boxes. Some of the horses demanded skill and attention to handle, and that saved their owners from my dialectics and me from their love-making. There was no use in a man offering me a horse that was moke enough for love-dawdling, and that's how that worked out.

Pa forbade fences. Ma said that unless I meant to marry one of the men it was foolish and unladylike to be riding about with them; they would have no respect for me. If I really was against marriage I'd have to take up some trade or profession; she wished she had been trained to something so that she could be independent and not be dragged in the backwash of man's mismanagement.

This brought me to consider my prospects and to find that I hadn't any. I loved to learn things—anything, everything. To attend the University would have been heaven, but expense barred that. I could become a pupil-teacher, but I loathed the very name of this profession. I should have had to do the same work as a man for less pay, and, in country schools, to throw in free of remuneration, the specialty of teaching all kinds of needlework. I could be a cook or a housemaid and slave all day under some nagging woman and be a social outcast. I could be a hospital nurse and do twice the work of a doctor for a fraction of his pay or social importance, or, seeing the tremendously advanced age, I could even be a doctor—a despised lady-doctor, doing the drudgery of the profession in the teeth of such prejudice that even the advanced, who fought for the entry of women into all professions, would in practice "have more faith in a man doctor". I could be a companion or governess to some woman appended to some man of property.

I rebelled against every one of these fates. I wanted to do something out of the ordinary groove. There *were* people who had done great things for the world, why not be one of such? Ma threw cold water on these haverings. Ma is the practical member of our ménage. She has to be, so that we have a ménage at all. Ma's thesis was that if all the millions who have gone have not improved the world, how was I going to do it in one slap? How would I start about it? Whereas, improvement seemed to me so simple that all that was needed was common sense and energy.

Pa was sympathetic. Ma says that I take after him, except when I am commendable. Pa has ever acknowledged the relationship with pride even during my most debbil-debbil stretches, which is very generous of Pa.

"There have been great women, haven't there, Pa?"

"Of course there have, and are, and will be again," said he.

21

"But what on earth makes you think you might be one of them?" demanded Ma.

"Why shouldn't she be?" murmured Pa.

"You can't be anything without means these days."

"The times are always the same. People make their opportunities."

"She doesn't strike me as that kind."

"Oh, I don't know," maintained Pa. "Greatness has sprung from unlikelier sources."

Chapter Three.

The Logic of Egotism.

Poverty is a stultifying curse. We suffered from it. Ma blamed Pa. Pa never blamed anyone but himself. He had not always been poor. He was no business man. Bad seasons and foolish investments lost him his parental station. Ma considered his term in Parliament as Member for Gool Gool his biggest financial mistake. Pa had been under heavy election expenses, and was robbed by a partner during his absence. Pa had had ambitions to improve the Colony through political action, and had failed. That was why Ma was alarmed by my symptoms. I was too young to remember Pa's Parliamentary term. Ma's abiding reference to it is that men are very fond of the sound of their own voices. Well, I like Pa's voice too, because it is never raised in blame.

Pa is tall and lean and lank and brown as is the ribbed sea sand, and he is fond of poetry. Byron is a favourite with him. He can quote Byron by the page.

This makes the madmen who have made men mad
By their contagion; conquerors and kings,
Founders of sects and systems, to whom add
Sophists, bards, statesmen, all unquiet things.
*   *   *   ***
He who surpasses or subdues mankind
Must look down on the hate of those below.

23

Such lines roll splendidly from him. Ma says a man betrays himself by what he extols. I asked if that also applies to women, but Ma says not nearly so accurately, as women have to pretend to like so many things to humour men.

Ma extols Dr. Watts. He is prosaic compared with Byron.

Not more than others I deserve,
Yet God has given me more
For I have food while others starve,
Or beg from door to door.

Which suggests mean favouritism on the part of God, and a priggish self-satisfaction on the part of one who has petty deserts.

Satan finds some mischief still for idle hands to do, has often driven me exasperated and frustrated from meditation when a thought was filling out like a sail catching a breeze.

Dr. Watts was the lighter side of Ma. She was also a whale on Shakespeare. I enjoyed him too, but Milton was too much of a good thing. Ma insisted that I should learn long slices of Milton as discipline and to elevate my thoughts.

Where joy for ever dwells; hail, horrors; hail,
Infernal world; and thou, profoundest hell,
Receive thy new possessor; one who brings
A mind not to be changed by place or time.
The mind is its own place, and in itself
Can make a heaven of hell, a hell of heaven.

"Bust" was the most ferocious expletive ever heard from women in Ma's family. It was considered the height of vulgarity and not allowed at all, really, but in the depths of some overpowering exasperation even Great-aunt Jane has been overheard expleting it. "Bust Milton!" I said many times to myself. "Paradise is lost surely enough while you have to be learning this stuff by heart."

The most interesting line in the book was, "Witness, William Yopp, Ann Yopp". They were a funny note in the stiff gilt-edged volume. Why had they a name like that? They were attached to the information that Mrs. Milton had got eight pounds for the twelve books of P.L. Poetry didn't seem to be a lucrative business, but of course that was over three hundred years ago, and to-day was different.

Ma said as I wasn't in a position to tackle professional training I must help Pa on the place. He could not afford to hire men. This brought me back to my idea of a career at the top where there was plenty of room above the tame-fowl openings, which were all that lay before one so poor and isolated. Ma said I should take stock of my possibilities and banish all silly delusions. Ma assisted in this stock-taking. She dwelt upon my lack of special gifts and said we should not shrink from unpleasant facts about ourselves, we must face them and grow strong. We must accept God's will without whining. It must be dreadful to have a daughter as disappointing as I am to Ma, and it is just as hard for such a fiasco of a girl to have a superb mother. I did not know which of the two trials was the heavier, but Ma did. Hers was the trial and mine the failure to take advantage of my heredity in her. However, life went on.

At that date there was a parliamentary election. FREE-TRADE or PROTECTION became a war cry. Pa was called upon to support the Member for our electorate.

'Possum Gully livened up. We had meetings at our house and I accompanied Pa on the rounds. There were young men everywhere all eager to argue politics with me. How I chafed that women were classed with idiots and children! Of course I should have had to wait until I was twenty-one to vote, but I longed to stand for Parliament then just as I was with my hair in a plat and my skirts above my ankles. I hankered to tackle the job of Premier for a start. The young men all said they would vote for me when I put up. Our Member was one of those who advocated extending the franchise to women, so I adored him and we were great friends. He said I was one of his best canvassers.

Scorning tame-hen accomplishments and lacking special gifts of God, which lift a person from obscurity to fame through an art, a sport, or an invention, I returned to the thought of general greatness. Pa was very proud when old campaigners said I was a chip of the old block. He was strenuously in favour of woman suffrage. Ma expostulated with him for taking me about. She said we soon would not have even a poor roof to cover us. My Grandma got to hear of me and wrote letters blaming Ma. When Great-aunt Jane next stayed with us she did her best to save me.

"You'll grow into one of those dreadful female agitators—eccentric women that men hate. You'll get the name of a man-hater if you don't take care."

"This men-hating business seems to be as lop-sided as God's will for women. You condemn a woman if she doesn't worship men. She is the one in the wrong to hate the darling creatures, though they're pretty hatable by all accounts. Then if a girl is fond of men that also disgraces her. I do like logic and fair play."

"So do I," interposed Ma, "but you'll have to resign yourself to it all being on the other side."

"It's all silly nonsense. The men don't act as if they hated me. The old ones as well as the boys all are friendly wherever I go."

"Men will always blather to a forward woman while she is young; but they won't respect her or marry her," said Aunt Jane.

"She couldn't marry more than one at a time, however willing she is," said Pa. "She has plenty of time yet."

When Pa and I were driving around the electorate together he talked about LIFE and said that my idea of being Premier was not fantastic. The political enfranchisement of women was inevitable, and women free could do what they liked with the world.

Votes for women was a magic talisman by which all evils and abuses were to be righted. Women no longer would have to pander to men through sexual attraction and pretend to be what they weren't. They would burgeon as themselves. Those were splendid days. Pa said I must educate myself in readiness as by the time I should be of age I could stand for Parliament and discover if I had ability as a statesman. As a beginning he suggested that I should study history and the lives of great people to learn how they conducted the business. To this end the poor dear once again postponed a new suit, which Ma truly said he needed to prevent his being mistaken for a scarecrow, and brought me home an armful of books, including some autobiographies.

That's how the trouble began.

The histories I left for later consumption, as the people

27

in them are always so long dead and are nearly all kings and queens and military or political murderers who have no relation to the ordinary kind of people like those I know in Australia. The biographies of real people nearer our own day, and especially the autobiographies, where people told about themselves, filled me with excitement.

Judging by the way Ma always misunderstands my deeds and purposes and intentions, and by what she and Aunt Jane tell me that other people do think or will think of me, it seemed that an autobiography was a device for disseminating personal facts straight from the horse's mouth.

I read ardently, nay, furiously would better express the way that one tackles the things one wants to do. Grace Darling, Charlotte Brontë, Joan of Arc and Mrs. Fry passed in review, evidently by dull old professors. These were a long time dead. Lives nearer to my own day had more appeal—until I read them. What I absorbed from autobiographies was not how to be great so much as the littleness of the great. Every one of those productions, whether the fiction that passes for reality or the decorated reality that is termed fiction was marred by the same thing —the false pose of the autobiographer.

Now, we are always warned against egotism as something more unforgivable, more unpopularising than vulgar sin. Yet everyone is a mass of egotism. They must be if they are to remain perpendicular. Henry Beauchamp later explained this to me. He says that little Jimmy Dripping is a much more important person to little Jimmy Dripping than the Prince of Wales is. If this were not so he says that the end of little Jimmy Dripping would soon be mud; that each fellow's self-importance is the only thing that

28

keeps him going. Well then, why make such an unholy fuss about egotism?

Ma despised egotism because she had none herself and happened by an accident to be perfect. Pa and I seemed to have whips and whips, but of the wrong kind. The best kind, the most profitable is like the hippo's epidermis. Another word for it is hide—HIDE. It works so that you think your own performance of sin or stupidity is quite all right, and only the other fellow's all quite wrong. Pa said that that kind of egotism was a magnificent battering ram for worldly success, but to have it you must be born without a sense of humour and without the ability to see yourself as others see you. I was beginning to suspect that a sense of humour was more profitable to the other fellow than to the owner.

The business of egotism needs to be regulated by give-and-take in real life or there would be general obstruction of all conversation and social intercourse, but that does not apply to an autobiography, at least not in conjunction with logic. The fact of an autobiography is in itself an egotism. People perpetrate autobiographies for the sole purpose of airing their own exploits. If they go off the track of displaying the writer they likewise cease to be autobiographies. Such documents are usually mawkishly egotistical instead of frankly so because they attempt the scientific impossibility of being unegotistical. Too, in autobiographies, the hero of the narrative tries to deprecate his goodness, while at the same time he often endeavours to depict himself as a saint worthy of wings. If he has a penny-dreadful parent he nevertheless paints himself as adoring him (or her) and by honouring one or both is a contestant for the doubtful prize of long life, which the bible promises people for enduring their immediate progenitors in any circumstances. (And I never could see in strict logic how that works.)

I have examined all available autobiographies since then but not one have I found by woman or man, scientist or simpleton, which did not assume the same pose. So little greatness did I find in the lives of the great as related by themselves that for a time I was diverted from the idea of becoming great myself by the notion of constructing a fictitious autobiography to make hay of the pious affectations of printed autobiographies as I know them.

Who has not read an autobiography beginning thus: "At the risk of being egotistical I must admit," etc. I determined to flout these pretences with an imitation autobiography that would wade in without apology or fear, biffing convention on the nose.

The days were goldenly long and warm, I was rabid for mental and physical action, and there was none in that state of discontent in which it had pleased God to place me. It makes me question His amiability in placing His victims. In addition to riding I swam in our weedy waterholes among leeches and turtles where there was also an occasional snake, but of mental pabulum there was no crumb to be found, except in books. I was a voracious reader, but after all, books pall on one when that one is throbbing to be doing something exciting. From 'Possum Gully to Spring Hill and round about to Wallaroo Plains there wasn't a real companion of my own age, nor any other age. The dissatisfaction of other girls stopped short at wondering why life should be so much less satisfactory to them than to their brothers, but they accepted it as the will of God. None of them was consumed with the idea of changing the world.

The idea of writing a book to make fun of the other books grew with cossetting. Ma said she had sufficient experience of my ideas to be chary of them. EXPERIENCE seems to stand by Ma like a religion.

Pa rubbed the top of his head contemplatively and said, "If you are man enough to write a book, I'll get you some paper."

"How could an untried girl write a book?" demanded Ma. "Why not start with a little story for the 'Children's Corner'? You can't run before you learn to walk."

CHAPTER FOUR.

"SATAN FINDS SOME MISCHIEF STILL."

A ream of paper is a large quantity to one who has never written a book nor met anyone who has done so—480 sheets all to myself.

"That'll hold you for a bit," said Pa.

"What a waste!" said Ma.

The pleasure of good penmanship on all that lovely white paper edged me on to begin upon my spontaneous career of slinging ink, of which this volume is to be the petite finale.

Ma admired classical features. Pa had them. Perhaps that is what misled her into a poor match, and why, no matter how often my looks are praised as lovely, she will not rank me as a beauty. She says such talk is to make a fool of me. So to be done with the uncertainty, I accept Ma's dictum that beauty lies in actions, and as my actions are all wrong, where could be my beauty? Nevertheless, bang went another convention. Men cared only for prettiness in girls, yet our house was a rendezvous for young men from all over the electorate and beyond it, who did not honestly come to talk politics with Pa, though they pretended that they did. I wasn't in danger of being embittered by a lack of admirers, nor of platonic men friends, as I was simple enough to think they were at the start. They teased me about dropping the Premiership and taking to writing.

32

Ma said there was no sight more nauseating than love-sick men all cackling and he-hawing and pretending they were angels who wouldn't let her pick up her thimble; while by-and-bye if I should marry one of them, most likely he would leave me to chop the wood and would turn her out of his house.

Pa said there was no use in quarrelling with NATURE or taking a jaundiced view.

Ma rejoined that EXPERIENCE had shown her that common sense was very rare.

It was a spring without a spring. The breezes had a strong dash of summer, but the cloudless skies looked down with an excess of that pitilessness which the Persian poet has advised us not to call upon. Not a speck the size of a man's hand came up for weeks to give even false hope, and the half-opened leaves withered on the rose bushes and orchard trees. The starving stock lacked strength to bring their young to birth, and the moan of dying creatures throughout that country side was a reproach to whatever power had placed them there. The earth was as dry as ashes. Isolated shrubs and plants, that had been the pride of settlers' drudging wives and daughters, died in spite of efforts to keep them alive with the slop water collected after household use. The wattle trees, however, because they were natives, were putting forth an unstinted meed of bloom with an optimism rivalling "God's in His Heaven, all's right with the world". Masses of lovely yellow fluff swayed to waves in the breeze and wafted perfume too chaste for the seventh heaven of oriental belief. This loveliness lacked competition in the grim landscape. I culled sprays to press between the leaves of some old book, and wondered would

33

there ever come a day when I should be as homesick for a bower of wattle bloom set in a frame of gumtrees as I was now wild to escape to other lands of castles and chateaux and Gothic cathedrals.

The drought made work in the garden superfluous. I had leisure to utilise that ream of paper. The burlesque autobiography grew apace. My idea of ridicule speedily enlarged as a reticule into which anything could be packed. I could express my longing to escape to other lands and far great cities across the sheening ocean to strange ports above and below the Line, where big ships and little go for their cargoes. It was an opportunity to crystallise rebellion and to use up some of the words which pressed upon me like a flock of birds fluttering to be let out of their cages. There is artistic satisfaction in liberating words: and they entered into me and flew from me like fairies.

It was absorbing to allot parts to characters. Uncertainty when to interpolate "Odds fish, ma'am," or "Gad Zooks," put me off a historical track, though I had started in an ancient castle on an English moor. I was also in a quandary about style, but at that time dear old Mr. Harris came to spend a few days with us prior to leaving the district. I let him into the secret. He was sympathetic in one way and discouraging in another. He said that the pursuit of literature was a precarious staff of life, but an engrossing hobby, if one had the leisure and the means. He asked me where the scene was set, a question I did not understand. He said if I would trust him to see the first chapter he could probably tell me.

We walked among the wattle blossom in the gully beyond the vegetable garden till we reached the top, where there were some rocks. We sat down, and he said, "My

34

dear Sybylla, I have read your beginning. Though imma-
ture it has promise."

I nearly stifled in agonised expectation of his condemnation. My whole feeling had come to the surface as sensitive as the nerve of a tooth. I knew he would never be
mean enough to tell Ma the full depth of my foolishness.

"Why do you write about a castle in England that you
have never seen?" he asked gently.

Without waiting for my reply he continued, "I'll tell
you, my dear little girl. The castle in England is a castle
in Spain, and 'tho' 'twas never built,' imagination makes
it more enthralling than things near at hand. Why not
try reality?"

I asked breathlessly what he meant.

"Well, instead of the roses on that castle wall, why not
this fragrant bower of wattle? Instead of the wind moan-
ing across the moor, why not the pitiless sun beating down
on the cracked dusty earth?"

"But that couldn't be put in a book—not in a story!"

"Why not, child?"

"Everyone knows that, and it is so tame and ugly."

"It would be most novel and informing to those who
are as familiar with the castle or a slum street as you
are with the wattles and the baked paddocks. Australia
is crying out to be done: England is done to death."

This was an expanding idea, like opening a window and
letting me look into a place I had not known before.

"You see, you know everyone in the Australian bush.
You could picture them with a vigor and conviction that
would be refreshing: and my dear, if you could project
yourself upon the canvas it would be most successful."

"Oh, I couldn't do that!" I shrank from this. "Besides, I have never done anything like the heroines in

novels. I am not sweetly good, and though Ma thinks I am possessed of a devil, I have never done anything really unrespectable. For example, I could never have been so unkind as to throw that dictionary back at the teacher like Becky Sharp did, though I *wish* I could do that kind of thing. It must be splendid."

"If you could draw portraits of all the characters that furnish your life it would be a good beginning."

"Oh, but I couldn't put in real people. They would not like to see themselves except as white-washed saints—like the yarns on the tombstones. I'd have to imagine people to make them interesting."

"Um!" said he, and then with a chuckle, "you go ahead. I shouldn't be surprised if they turn out to be more real that way. But there is one thing, my dear, be Australian. It is the highest form of culture and craftmanship in art to use local materials. That way you stand a chance of adding to culture. The other way you are in danger of merely imitating it, and though imitation is a form of flattery to the imitated, it is a form of weakness or snobbery in the perpetrator. You must find your own way and your own level. The material is in you: all that is required is industry in cultivation."

I could hardly wait till the end of his visit to plaster the ideas he had put into my head upon the original burlesque. Ma said that Mr. Harris was right to a certain extent, that to pretend to be what one was not was the height of vulgarity, but she couldn't see that an interesting book could be made of reality: it was dreary enough to live in the bush in drought time: no one could possibly find any pleasure in reading about such misfortune.

Ma always brings up EXPERIENCE. She has often

routed Pa from the field of philosophy with the records of EXPERIENCE, and she now inquired what was the sense in wasting time and paper in this way? Why not do something practical? Pa though, is always willing to believe that the latest venture must be better than the preceding.

I set out to do the equivalent of taking two photographs on the one plate. I was to burlesque autobiography and create the girl of my admiration, and fill in with a lot of lifelike people as a protest against over-virtuous lay figures. One thing I have always envied in girls is the ability to fly into a towering rage. At school there were two bad-tempered dunces and they enjoyed my brain effort. I lived in terror of their temper and did their sums with alacrity. Poor Old Harris was careful not to stir them up, and they did pretty well what they liked. So my heroine was to be the antithesis of conventional heroines. All my people were to be created in the image of reality—none of them bad enough to be tarred and feathered, none good enough to be canonised. But people are never what they think themselves, and by the results which accrued it would seem that it is equally difficult to present a character as you intend.

Up to that date I do not remember being so fully interested in anything. I had a secret delight. I ceased to talk about it even to Pa. He and I had quite opposite tastes in stories. He liked adventure: Mayne Reed, Fenimore Cooper, Captain Marryat, Gil Blas, Rider Haggard, but I had one or two of George Gissing's books, Vanity Fair, Colonel Newcome and Esther Waters, and enjoyed that style. No, I could not write dashingly enough to interest Pa. Ma was reading an annotated edition of Shakespeare, and that took her above my sphere of effort.

Bewitchment shadowed the paper as I progressed. I could not do what I liked with the people. I often found them as troublesome as Ma found me, and I think in the end they made rather a pie of my theme, though I did not know it at the time. The book was a companion as well as an entertainment, a confidant and a twin soul: You know how a piece of lace that you have made yourself has a charm lacking in a much better piece made by someone else? So with that book. I used to climb on the hay in the shed behind the stables on Sunday afternoons and read it over—like doing all the parts in a play myself, though at the time I had not seen a play. I must have had a lot of ingrowing egotism, and it came out in this way as the pimples or boils that are common to boys.

I was sardonically amused to depict that reality suggested by Mr. Harris.

Our home was of wood and of the usual pattern and situation in a particularly ugly portion of the bush. We were dished in a basin of low scrubby ranges which are familiar to the poorer settlers where the fertile patches are land-locked in a few big holdings by hard-headed fellows who got in early with capital and grants and convicts.

Instead of hedges we had dog-leg and brush fences, and stumps in the cultivation paddocks. There were fowl-houses covered with tin to render them safe against sharp-snouted spotted marsupial cats; the mess-mate roosting trees also had wide rings of tin around the trunks to save the turkeys by night. Cowsheds were roofed with stringy-bark. Fields of briars and rugged ranges were all around; a weedy water hole in the middle; the not-yet-bleached bones of beasts were a common decoration. No roofs but our own were within sight. It was a raw contrast to the

English scenery on which I doted, with its thatched cottages, trailing roses, gabled farm houses, towered ancestral halls with Tudor chimneys amid oaks and elms and cawing rooks and moors and downs, wolds, woods, spinneys and brooks. Such reality as mine would look mighty queer in a book, something like a swaggie at a Government House party, but it was as easy to describe as falling off a log.

The people belonging to this scenery were so ordinary and respectable and decent that a yarn about them could not possibly attract the attention of a reader. The probability of readers must have popped up somewhere along the track. I had had no thought of them when I started. I'm sure nothing but genius could make the 'Possum Gully kind of reality interesting, and as I am only a jokist I had to bring out the paintpot of embellishment to heighten or lower the flat colorless effect.

There are times when our own case is so blinding that we are unable to feel or to see outside it. We are shut within ourselves. Sometimes these moods are merry and sometimes sad, but always self-sealed. If merry, so all-sufficient is our hilarity that grey skies or black nights have no power to damp our inward fire. But let us be sad, and the brilliance of the sun seems callous. We cannot reach outside ourselves. When young we demand so much that is beyond us that the first lessons in EXPERIENCE are the hoeing of the chastening row of disappointment.

I had a fever which fed upon itself like the green-eyed monster, and it was a great relief to be shedding it like a snake-skin. A desire to have someone to read the result came upon me towards the end. I don't know whether this was gregariousness or mere egotism, like my cat's when she brings home a kitten and dumps it for us to see. I was more selective than the cat. She doesn't pick her appreciators. She drops her kitten among us regardless of passing boots, and also regardless of who may be in the boots. I adore her and indulge her and so have been surprised that she did not bring me her kitten.

I was more demanding. I wanted someone who would understand. Who better than our greatest Australian author? I quite understood him since ever I was old enough to lisp a line of his ballads, what more sequential than his understanding of me? In the innocence of my heart, or it may have been the heartlessness of my innocence, I confidently sent him the manuscript. Having worshipped at his shrine with a whole-heartedness which we can enjoy but once in life, I felt sure of welcome within the gates of his interest.

In those days so entire was my unsophistication that I did not suspect that an author, even the AUSTRALIAN GREATEST, may not have earned thousands by his pen, and may be pestered by so many literary duds that he sees each fresh one draw near with weariness and terror.

To escape making a short story long, my idol welcomed my attempt with cheers for its ORIGINALITY, and asked would I trust him with the manuscript?

WOULD I ! ! ! ! !

I'd have given him any or all of my treasures, even my black-dappled-grey filly, a doll, a book of girls' stories or a little box covered with velvet and sea shells. When I come to think of it, these were my only treasures, and he could not take the filly with him to London whither he was going. I was excited by his acceptance of the manuscript. I once gave Ma a little story for her birthday. She thanked me, but did not look as if it were an enjoyable present, and never said whether she read it before burning it under the copper. I hoped the great Australian writer would read my offering before burning it, as I had taken pains to write it nicely—no blots or scratchings-out.

CHAPTER FIVE.

FINISHING SCHOOL.

This matter of the autobiography settled with satisfaction, I regained my chronic distaste for the kind of
life into which it had pleased God to stuff me. The entertainment of fashioning my characters and acting their
parts gave me the idea of being an actress. Acting appeared to be the only avocation open to a girl who was
not a musical genius nor trained in anything but domesticity. Heaven knows why I had such a notion, for I
loathed hypocrisy, and in my circle, acting was another
name for this. I had never seen a play nor a mummer,
nor even read one—a play I mean—except Shakespeare's.
It must have been the delirium of day-dreaming. Fantasy.

My delirium escaped me one day and really startled poor
Ma. We had a State child called Eustace to help about
the place, or hinder, Ma said. He had once been an
elephant's leg in a school play in Goulburn and considered
it a great lark. I concocted a scene, in which I was to
accidentally fight a duel with him. He refused to fight
unless I wore trousers. I put on Pa's, but Eusty said
Odds Fish, no dashing blade would fight with such a
spectacle. So I tried a pair of Eusty's in which I showed
a bit of knee like a fat boy. Eusty called me Greedy
Guts. We staged the drama in the hay shed. Pa was
concerned that we might have set alight to the straw.
Ma said never, never let her hear of me again putting on

42

trousers; showing my person, failing in self-respect before a State School boy!

My defence was that to act Shakespeare (whom everyone respects next to the bible), I should have to don doublet and hose. Me acting SHAKESPEARE! Ma was shocked to discover such foolishness in me. I must really be mad. This put me in a fantod so that Ma reported me to Pa and threatened to enlist the clergyman to exorcise the devil in me.

"Now," said Pa, when left to rebuke me, "you must be careful not to upset your mother. The game is not worth the candle." The only thing wrong in the affair was that I had upset Ma: I must never upset Ma: she was a wonderful woman.

"She is not always right just because she is my mother," I grumbled.

"The law is that the Queen can do no wrong," said Pa.

"Yes, but a Queen is a being raised to false majesty."

"Have you forgotten that a woman's kingdom is the home?"

Pa had a twinkle in his eyes, but I refused to melt. EXPERIENCE was certainly teaching me that a sense of humour is too often an advantage to the one who hasn't it. A lack of a sense of humour, like a lack of good-temper, can be used as a waddy.

Later Ma upbraided Pa because he had not severely trounced me. Pa said, "I see nothing wrong with the child's intellect except that it is too bright for its uses".

"If she comes to harm, you must take the consequences," said Ma. "I find her with a boy—swept up from the gutter or somewhere—in a pair of trousers exposing her flesh."

"Eustace is a fine boy. He only needs a chance."

"A chance to get into mischief and laziness. Dear me, where would a child of mine get notions of the stage—the lowest . . . "

Pa began to rub his hair gently on end and remarked, "I suppose a sea bird reared in the middle of a desert would retain aquatic tendencies."

"She does not take after my side of the house," said Ma.

She was too perturbed about my aberration, as she called it, to leave me to Pa. She "took me in hand". I resented the evil she discerned in me, felt that she was unfair, but there was no appeal against Ma. She disabused my mind of any notion that I could go upon the stage. She ridiculed my every feature and every contour. Ma believes in finishing things. She says it is a sign of a weak mind to begin things and leave them half done. Ma has no weakness of mind. She always finishes the hardest task. She finished me to squashation like a sucked gooseberry. I often longed for death or a nunnery as an escape from my depressing lack of desirable attributes.

But I was freed from notions. Never again would I have the conceit and delusions to think of the stage. Never would I have the effrontery to seek any but the humblest jobs. Should anyone flatter me I would know them for what they were at the first soft word. Ma had ensured me against making a fool of myself by attempting flights, but she had not helped me towards contentment. The native wombat role for me henceforth. Those who are low need fear no fall. I had always jeered at the Blackshaws, our neighbours, by saying they would never make fools of themselves and by adding that those who had not enough stuffing to make fools of themselves at times would never make anything else of themselves.

The finishing stroke in Ma's finishing school was the

44

threat to report me to the nice little clergyman. I loved him dearly. Like Old Harris he was an outlet. I was so worked up that I warned Ma that I'd listen to what she told him. Ma said it was a grave pass to be dictated to in her own house by a creature she had brought into the world. She demanded an apology. I refused. If I expressed contrition to Pa all was washed out, but with Ma it was different. She said penitent gush was useless without reform in deeds. Ma was what she called consistent.

The clergyman came next day, and after dinner, when Pa was at the stables feeding his horses, I loitered in the passage to hear what Ma was saying. Sure enough, she was reporting me as an abnormal specimen. I was infuriated, but the clergyman's voice, in the tone of the Collects—perhaps it was the Twentieth Sunday after the Melbourne Cup—said, "But my dear Mrs. Melvyn, I cannot see anything wrong at all. That child has such glorious eyes that when they are fixed upon me I always find I can preach a better sermon."

"She can be nice when she wants to."

"Adolescence is a difficult time. You might let her come with me around the parish and to stay with my wife and daughters till I come next month. During our progress I could find time to talk to her on spiritual things: and I get so tired of driving, and she is such a clever whip."

That was one in the eye of Ma. I was as gay as a lark, and a willy-wagtail or two thrown in, when serving supper. I awaited breathlessly to hear the results of the clergyman's championship. Disillusion awaited me.

There was only a thin partition between my bed and Ma's, and I could always hear Ma's final injunctions to

45

Pa. Tonight Pa opened the discourse. "Mr. David wants to take Sybylla with him."

"So he said." Ma's voice was a drought of common sense.

"Are you letting her go?"

"I am not."

"Can't you spare her?"

"Not to Mr. David."

"Why?"

"Why should I let her run around with that silly old man?"

"He's not so silly."

"All men are silly where there is a young girl."

"I think you carry suspicion too far," murmured Pa.

"His cloth doesn't protect a man from being blind to faults in a girl, though he would be dull to the problems of older women."

Pa gave a loud grunt. In a little while Ma complained, "I wish you wouldn't snore so". Pa hadn't begun yet, so Ma was taking time by the forelock, as she often adjured me to do.

I lay awake pondering her words. Surely a clergyman, and such a nice lean helpless-looking little one as Mr. David, would not be guilty of flattery or trying to make a fool of me; and he wasn't a bit like the pretentious Canon, who had once taken Mr. David's place. Now, if it had been the Canon! I remember chortling when I read the table of consanguinity beginning, "A man may not marry his grandmother," but Pa had said that human nature was such that . . . well, such daunting things are attributed to human nature that one would prefer to be one of the higher animals and have decent instincts.

I had a good yarn with Mr. David on his next visit.

I had him alone because a neighbour who was ill sent for Ma, and Pa had driven her over. I confessed one thing that prejudiced me against God was that He had to be fed on everlasting praise. I had to grow strong on disapprobation, but God had to be praised unceasingly by measley creatures which He Himself had made. The Psalms were ridiculous with fulsome praise. Egotism in me had to be stemmed and denied, but God seemed to be a sticky mess of it. Another reason I could not respect God was that it seemed so despicable to continually spy upon distressed little girls for the purpose of condemnation.

Mr. David chuckled and said, "Poor God: He has need of young minds like yours to think their way to Him, not to rebel against Him. He needs your help to free Him from all the stupid misrepresentation. Sybylla, m'dear, God is aching for your loving help."

The problem was thrown on me in a way that had never even been hinted in 'Possum Gully by anyone except Pa, and his theories were discredited by Little Jimmy Dripping's common sense.

This devastating idea haunted me day and night. The God made by disagreeable and selfish old men in their own image and erected as a bogey to control women and children retreated before it. Was there no God, only as He was made manifest by nobility and truth in ourselves? This idea, at first releasing, grew to be terrifying. It left one lost and alone. The European God with all His masculine bullying unfairness was at least something to be sure of, however unsatisfactory. No God except as we demonstrate Him! Whew! There was a burden too difficult and demanding to be borne. No wonder people evaded such a vast responsibility by hypocrisy, or sought less exacting conceptions of God in josses which could be placated by praise and candles and incense and other material bribes. It was a sobering revelation.

However, LIFE went on.

I loathed 'Possum Gully more and more. The horses were dog-poor. To ride them at the beginning of a bleak and droughty winter would have been wanton cruelty plus extravagance. March was crisp and cool, with a hint of frost which makes one feel as strong as a young colt, and I rebelled against the continual shining of pot lids, the unnecessary whitening of the hearth, just because Ma insisted upon being the top-notcher.

I took to the piano. Ma said that hard work and worry had driven piano-playing out of her. I said why not turn it the other way about, and drive out dullness with the piano, but Ma preferred to excel in spotless floors and windows. My thumping on the piano irritated her as a love of idleness, and I had to desist.

I hated every bit of the life but the sunsets and moonlight and the wild flowers. The watch-dog's bark was often the only incident of the day with its promise of a caller to break monotony. Sometimes this would be a tea agent or a stock inspector. The regular visitors were Mrs. Olliver, Mrs. Blackshaw, or Mrs. Crispin come to spend the afternoon. I resented their inadequacy as society. It was not their fault. I loved them warmly, much more than they loved me, I am sure, and did more for them than they did for me, because I was something for them to criticise and cackle about. "That Sybylla does this and that." Someone was always reporting what the other said, and that annoyed Ma. Pa said rubbish, if criticism was sifted out of conversation people would be silent from Goulburn to Bourke and Broken Hill and beyond.

Poverty can make pioneering a sorry job. In any case it has always been heavier on women than on men. 'Possum Gully was a generation or two removed from frontier pioneering, though Australia never had a frontier. She had an outback which became back paddocks with familiarity. But all the trying part and none of the adventure of pioneering remained at 'Possum Gully. The inconvenient houses depending on the main strength of drudgery, the absence of comfort or beauty or any cultural possibilities or opportunities for self-development were still enough to induce Back Blocks lunacy in any one above a cow in ability.

Those good ladies all had large families, and their conversations were about recipes for cakes and puddings and little Tommies' tummyaches, and then boasting bees as to who skinned her hands the most in washing her husband's trousers of moleskin. They and their daughters, following in their tracks, were held up to me as admirable. Horrors! Broken down drudges talking of uterine troubles and the weariness of child-bearing! I could not accept that as the fullness of life from any God worthy of worship or gratitude. These martyrs to stupidity were extolled in sententious tones as "mothers of families". They were populating Australia. I said that instead of Ned Crispin and others I should prefer Australia to remain populated by kangaroos and the dear little bears and kangaroo rats that were as thick about us as sheep. This was the sort of thing that made me entertaining to the 'Possum Gullyites, and troubled Ma.

Another winter wore away and a bit of a spring deluded the land. We had saved a few hundred sheep, and wool

49

would be scarce because so many sheep had died. Just as shearing was coming on Pa had a call from an old colleague to help fight a by-election in Junee. This was a key electorate on Pa's side, and he said he could not let the country down. The shearing would take only a few days, and Mr. Blackshaw offered to oversee it. He too saw the importance of Junee being saved for the right side.

This infuriated poor Ma. She said Pa might as well have been a drunkard who went on the booze at critical times. To leave our sole income to the superintendence of an outsider was not merely undignified, it was lunacy. Ma said I could now see why she tried to save me from my father's tendencies. She held that a man should first save his home and family, and the country could come second. Pa said if the country was not saved for the homes and liberty Australia might as well be under the Russian Czars.

At any rate Pa went, ran away in a crisis, Ma said, just because he loved to hear himself spouting on a platform. Ma said I would never understand what she had suffered, that life was a bitter thing with a useless husband. I ventured to say that Pa didn't have such a slashing life either. Ma maintained it was much harder for her, but that I could not understand that.

I was piqued by this accusation of lack in understanding. I said I could understand it was easier for Pa because he was so proud of her and thought her so wonderful. He at least had the satisfaction of thinking what a stroke he had done to choose and win such a wife, while she must always be ashamed of herself for marrying so much beneath her; but that did not appease Ma. Quite the opposite. Quite, quite the opposite! I gathered that

Ma had the added affliction of me as a daughter, which couldn't matter so much to Pa because I took after him.

Then Mr. Blackshaw's back was smitten and he could not rise from bed. All the men at one time or another had a bad back. It was Mr. Blackshaw's turn. Ma was a deserted heroine.

"It is my turn to save the ship," said I. "You always say that I'll have to help Pa. I know how to pick up and roll a fleece, and Eusty can be tar boy and rouse-about."

This did not dispose of the pressing. We had a hand-worked press of Pa's construction which Ma said showed what a helpless botcher Pa was, but all the neighbours used to borrow it, which further shows the standard of the neighbourhood, or that Pa wasn't so bad.

We turned the hayshed into a floor for two men with blades, who wanted to learn so that they could go down the Riverina next year. The skilled shearers had not yet returned to their little homes in the wallaby scrubs around us. These lads had to do their own work and come a distance each morning and they were very slow. All this prolonged the festival.

Ma vetoed the idea of my working in the shed. It would have been fun and a relief from the pot lids and d'oyleys. (It sometimes took half an hour to iron one of the prevalent d'oyleys.)

"You would be talked about," said Ma, "and the boys would be giggle-gaggling with you instead of attending to their work."

She decided to attend to the shearing herself and let me do the cooking. This was a disappointment, as to press one's face into a nice fat sheep all white from the shears is a delight. The two shearers were selectors' sons in their teens. We knew each other minutely, but did

51

not "associate". We were a grade higher socially, but had we shown it they would not have shorn for us, and would have slanged us throughout the neighbourhood. Ma and I managed to be too busy to sit down to meals with them, and thus was a gradation of the caste system preserved.

The shearing was saved but the country was lost in so far as Pa's man was rejected by the electors, and Pa did not have his election expenses paid.

CHAPTER SIX.

THE BREAD OF THE MAIL BOX RETURNS.

The mail was left three times a week in a battered kerosene can nailed on the fence of the main road two miles away — that is if the mailman was not too drunk to sort it. He liked to keep any special letter a day or two till he read it and then gummed it up again. Other times he was content with tearing a corner off so that he could look in. He enlivened monotony by a lively interest in his neighbours' doings.

I was always hopeful of the mail. I don't know why, for the mail box only gives back the fruit of what is sown in it, and I had nothing to sow. It was at least a channel of possibility, a Tattersall's sweep that might throw up a prize, and I hungrily devoured the news of the great, reported in the newspapers.

There was no hope of any eruption in 'Possum Gully, it would need to be an irruption. There was no public road nearer than two miles. There was no stream to attract anglers, nor scenery for a painter, nor rocks for a geologist. My chiefest grudge against it has always been its ugliness. It is ragged rather than rugged, and lacks grandeur. We are too much in the ranges for them to be blue. They are merely sombre. The one glory that I 'dote and gloat on is the sunset. I love the sinking sun red as a fire between the trunks of the trees upon the hillside, and by running a quarter of a mile up the track can catch the afterglow of the grandeur of transfigured clouds on a more distant horizon.

Great was my astonishment one dull day to find a letter and a large parcel both addressed to me, and with English stamps. The letter had the corner torn off but not enough to divulge the contents. The parcel had been untied, but I was so surprised that I was not resentful of this. In all my life I had not received so much as a post card written by a hand in another country. I had no idea of the what and why of the parcel, but I trembled with excitement. I galloped part of the way home and in a little gully where the hop scrub was thickest got off to investigate.

The parcel was books. Oh, joy! Had old Harris gone back to England without letting us know? But they were all the same book. Each had the same picture on the cover. I had never seen so many of one book except school readers. And the title of the book was my spoof autobiography — and there was my name printed below it ! ! ! ! It looked so different in print — so conspicuous somehow, that I was frightened.

The letter was from a man I did not know, a business letter, as his name was printed at the top of the stationery. This gentleman wrote that herewith under separate cover he had pleasure in sending me six presentation copies of my novel with the publishers' compliments. He would be glad to have my acknowledgment in due course.

There in the hop scrub I faced the biggest crisis I have known to date. What on earth was I to do about this? What would Ma say? It was a shock that this thing written as a lark could come back to me as a real book like one written by a grownup educated person. I never in the world thought of an author as resembling myself, not even the feminine ones.

There was a dreadful fascination in peeping between the leaves. There it all was, all my irreverence about God and parents, and the make-believe reality that I had piled on with a grin in a spirit of "I'll show 'em reality as it is in 'Possum Gully." I never had a book affect me like this one. It was as if the pages were on fire and the printing made of quicksilver. Was this because I knew what was in it, or was it just plain egotism, which no decent girl should have? I wished now that I had written a ladylike book that I could be pleased with. If only I had known it would be printed I should have done so. Those poor lost girls who have a baby without being married must feel like I did. There would be the baby but all the wild deep joy of it would be disgrace and trouble.

I thought of dropping the packet near home so that I could burn the books one by one secretly, but the mailman had opened them. He would ask Pa. No, I must face it. Ma and Pa were waiting for me, as I was late, and everyone looked forward to the mail, though the crop that Pa put in it mostly bore no fruit but bills.

Pa reached for the packet while Eusty took old Bandicoot's bridle.

"What's this?" asked Pa.

Ma came forward. She and Pa and Eusty each seized a book. Eusty and Pa regardless of evening jobs, there and then opened theirs.

"Golly!" screeched Eusty, inspecting the picture on the cover. "Is that meant to be you on old Bandicoot? Bandicoot looks as if he is going to have a foal, and you look as if you are going to fall off and your clothes blow up!"

"I don't understand this," said Ma dubiously. "Some confidence trick man must have got hold of you. How did this book get to the printer?"

55

I explained that I had sent my ream of paper, when written upon to the GREATEST AUSTRALIAN AUTHOR, and he had asked me to let him keep it, and I thought it was only to read.

"Your father will be getting a big bill for this, and we'll be ruined. I wonder how much it has cost to print all this trash — it might be twenty pounds, or even fifty. You'll find EXPERIENCE a bitter and expensive teacher, but you must pay the price of your own wilfulness. What is hard and unjust is that I have continually to be paying it with you."

"This is like a meteor falling in the paddock, let us investigate it," said Pa.

Ma said, first things first; she must prepare the evening meal while I put the chooks to bed safe from the native cats: we couldn't all chase the shadow while the substance escaped us.

Eusty speedily arrived at his opinion. He had no impediment to arriving at his opinion on any subject. Old Harris said that Eusty was a perfect example of the cocksure Australian youth, possessed of the irreverence which resulted from lack of culture.

"I reckon this is a slashing lark," he grinned. "And crikey, if it doesn't get people's nark up, I'm a goanna with two tails." Eusty further expressed himself as full up of it, as it was only a blooming girl's book, and went about his jobs.

Pa wiped his pince-nez and looked thoughtfully into space and murmured half to himself, "Of course you are not to blame for inexperience, but it's a very strange thing. I am tremendously interested in what you have done, but you must not expect anyone else to be. It has just a local interest because you make things seem so true, even things that have no relation to anyone we know, that it is like a looking glass. I really had no idea that you had anything like this in your head. It would have been wiser to consult me beforehand; I could have saved you disappointment."

With his kindness to anyone in a scrape, he added, "You must try again and write something adventurous. Authors write many books before they succeed, so you needn't worry that no one will take any notice of you. I have sometimes thought of describing the old pioneer life that is fast disappearing, but when I came to put pen on paper something always interrupted, or the experiences seemed such small potatoes compared with the Spanish Main or American pioneering, that they could not carry interest beyond those who actually knew them."

Ma made sure that the pigs and fowls had been fed, the calves penned, the flowers watered, and kindling gathered ready for the morning fire before she read her copy.

She said she was relieved that it was not as bad as she had expected, for how could a girl without EXPERIENCE write a book? She said it was lacking in discretion to have rung in such peculiar characters. There would be unpleasantness with worthy people who would think themselves ridiculed. She also said it was unfilial to concoct an uncomplimentary exaggerated fabrication in such a way that outsiders would think it represented Pa and her. This was very mild and very handsome of Ma, but she is superb in a real crisis, though often irritating in a trivial rumpus. And what kind of a mad notion was it to rig up such a headstrong unladylike girl to be mistaken for myself? Ma said it was hard enough for a girl whose father could not provide for her, without handicapping herself with false reports. I was in danger of being put down as unwomanly, and men liked none but womanly girls. I shall never be a lady and poor Ma will never be anything else. So I plucked up to contend that it was womanized girls that men craved, and that it did not matter what men thought of me, as what I thought of them would even things up. "What nonsense you talk," said Ma, "You will find that in this world men have it all their own way. We won't waste any more time on the silly book at present. I only hope it doesn't involve us in any expense. The publishers must have little to do, or a peculiar taste. Put the copies away where no one will see them. A nine days wonder soon fades."

I sent a copy to Old Harris. He wrote that it was surprising to see such a novel issuing from the stately house of McMurwood — this alone assured my status. "But my dear girl, I am troubled by the tenor of the book. Where is your radiance, your joyous sense of fun, your irrepressible high spirits? The pages seethe with discontents and pain. Have you been living alone in your spirit, suffering as we who had deepest affection for you did not dream? This distresses me. I cannot recognise you at all in these pages. Why not set our hearts at ease with a companion volume in which you give us your bright and illuminating self?"

Pa said Old Harris was a wonderful man. Ma said how was a man wonderful who had wasted all his opportunities. Pa said that Mr. Harris had understanding.

"Humph!" said Ma. "All men, and the older they grow the sillier they are, *understand* a young woman, but a mature mother of a family or an old woman burdened to the earth with real griefs and troubles — thrust upon her by other people — could drop under their feet without attention."

58

Pa said that it was useless to quarrel with NATURE. And that was the end of the book. We got on with the drought. It was a hummer that year and took all our attention.

Chapter Seven.

"That Sybylla!"

It wasn't the end of the book after all. Because of the drought, and the horses being poor, visiting among the neighbours practically ceased, and it was some time before we knew what was going on. We were further like ostriches, because hard times had suspended our subscriptions to the papers.

Eusty went to Stony Flat — the neighboring community centring in a school — with the Stringybark Hill boys who were meeting in a picnic and football match, and he came home with a briar bush of gossip.

"Golly, Sybylla, you've done it this time, I reckon," announced he. "Everybody is snake-headed about your blooming old book."

"Where did they get it?" asked Ma. My heart missed a beat in dismay.

"Old Foxall can't keep enough on hand. They must have printed dozens more than those you had. Golly, I'm glad I'm not you. All the old blokes despise you and laugh at the idea of you trying to write a book."

"That reminds me," said Pa. "The other day when I went over to Blackshaw, he got as red in the face as if he had been popping his brand on my sheep, and hid a book behind his back. I knew what it was, as he never read another book in his life, I'll swear. Poor old chap, he apologised and said he would put it on the fire, that he

60

only got it to see if it was as wicked as people were saying. At any rate, my girl, you've made people read a book for the first time in their lives."

"What did you say?" inquired Ma.

"I told him that a marvellous thing had happened in our midst, and they were too ignorant to know it. Then he got squiffy and thanked God that *his* daughters were different. It appears that the Wesleyan preacher last Sunday denounced you. He said that your attitude towards religion damns you."

"People are magging more about your book than the drought or the price of wool," chimed Eusty. "Everybody is sorry for your Pa and Ma. They say you should have been kept under more."

"Now you see what your policy of encouraging her has done," said Ma.

"Agh! A lot of magpies chattering on the fence posts."

I was in an agony of disgrace. I did not sleep that night. I lay awake shivering with ignominy and listening to the mopokes and plovers. I did not mind what people thought or were so silly as to mis-think about me, it was Ma. To have brought disgrace upon her and to be compelled to remain there and be tied to it in 'Possum Gully was a deadly tribulation.

A prophet denounced where he is known often has a great innings among strangers. Sometimes things are thus and sometimes otherwise. In my case it was both thus and otherwise. Otherwise came later: I must continue about thus.

Following his next sorties Eusty reported that Mrs. Crispin had said to Mrs. Oxley that she had not been to see poor Mrs. Melvyn, as she did not know what to say about that Sybylla. "Then they cackled," said Eusty,

61

"and said something more about *that Sybylla* which I couldn't hear."

"I'm sure that was no fault of your ears," remarked Pa, and smiled to himself. I wondered why. I thought it callous of Pa.

Ma took the whole thing calmly. She was disapproving but that was business as usual.

At anyrate Eusty had great pleasure in the affair. His eyes popped and he danced a can-can after each report. "You've done it, Sybylla," he would giggle. "All the girls reckon they ain't going to talk to any one so unwomanly. Elsie Blinder says her Ma says it is indelicate for a girl to write books at all."

The trouble spread. It seemed to be more wide-spread than the drought, which that season was confined to the Southern Tableland. People arrived to condole with Pa about his hussy of a daughter, and had to scrunch on the brakes when they found Pa so lost to all 'Possum Gully and Little Jimmy Dripping common sense as to be vainglorious. He enjoyed being my father much more than I enjoyed being myself.

Every house in the district had the book, though hitherto the only reading had been the *"Penny Post"* and the Bible or a circular from Tattersall's. It was the sensation of the age and at least relieved dulness. People in other 'Possum Gullies were equally excited, and not so annoyed. The mail bag grew fuller and fuller with the weeks. Girls from all over Australia wrote to say that I had expressed the innermost core of their hearts. Others attacked Pa for allowing his daughter to write such a book. As one man put it, "Malicious lies without cause, for it is not a bit like us." Another wrote, "Of course she has altered little things here and there but everybody who reads the book

62

will immediately know it is us because it is all so plain and true to life."

Pa seemed to enjoy these outbursts. I could not see why. I was unnerved to have enraged people whom I had not thought of when writing, as well as others that I had not even heard of.

"You must answer these letters," said Pa. "It will give you a balanced sense of responsibility."

I had to chew my pen for quite a time. I wrote humbly that I had not known the specific people but had meant simply to make fun of general reality. Pa said it was a generous letter, that it could not do any harm, neither would it do any good.

So I read the copies and then something came up in me and I jabbed down a postscript: "I don't know you and am sorry that you are angry, but if the cap fits you and you make a noise and wear it, I can't help it."

There was no reply to these letters.

Other letters to Ma put the cap on. The one from Grandma was a sizzler. To me she wrote that she had hoped her eyelids would be closed in death before such a disgrace had been brought upon her, but she did not blame me so much as my mother.

Ma got another letter, from an old neighbour when we had lived up the country, pitching into her and accusing her of aiding me in making fun of him because Ma had always been stuck up because she was a swell, and thought her family better than his.

It was dreadful that Ma, the one perfect member of our ménage, who was beautiful and good and clever, who had sacrificed her life for Pa and me, should have this to bear.

"I knew there was something wrong," she remarked.

"There has been no one near the place to borrow so much as a bottle of yeast or half a hundred of flour for weeks."

Ma is the most wonderful housekeeper in the district. The result is that the neighbours for miles around come to her when they want anything. They send to her when there is an accident, and more than once she has set an arm or leg in such a way that the doctor coming later has highly commended her skill and left it untouched. She can make dresses like a picture, and her pastry is so light and flaky that Pa says one needs a nosebag to keep it from flying away during consumption. Her bread is always taken for that of the best bakery, and so on, and so on. It is a sore trial for Ma to have such a poor husband, but added to that having her daughter, whom she had hoped would be a comfort, turning out to be a wolf in the barn, was indeed tragedy for Ma. It wasn't any pleasure to me, but I had brought it on myself. It was right that I should suffer, but Ma was suffering through no fault of her own. She was a genuine heroine.

I had to be utterly discredited. I stated that no one had known a thing about my writing a book. Pa was inculpated as far as supplying the paper, but had not suspected what I was to write. Ma was very generous and kind to everyone who complained. She wrote them nice letters explaining she entirely disapproved of me, that she had known nothing of my intentions, was grieved by my wicked wilfulness, which never came from her either by precept or example, and that she herself was the greatest victim to be mistaken for the mother in the foolish autobiography. "But ma," I said, "I made up a woman with no resemblance to you on purpose, it is not my fault."

But of course denial would not adjust matters It showed the abnormal power of what was printed, and was my first inkling that what was printed could be wide of the facts. EXPERIENCE taught me that, but those who had never tried to write anything but a letter could not learn by experience.

"If the child had known enough to take a *nom-de-plume,* her relatives and friends would have been able to remain silent when she failed and to boast if she succeeded, without this pillaloo," said Pa. Parliament had taught him about human nature.

I lay awake night after night wondering what I could do. I made up my mind to commit suicide so that Ma could be rid of me, but when I had worked myself up to it one day, Pa asked me to help him draft and brand a flock of sheep, and it was such a relief that instead of suiciding I decided to run away. Even that was not immediately practicable as I hadn't a railway fare, and if I left, Pa would not have had anyone to help with the place. I helped reap our bit of wheat that year, with a hook, and I milked the cows, so that Eusty could help Pa top the fences in the back paddock. I was awfully glad to keep to my own back yard. I did not want to give the girls the satisfaction of fumigating society by cutting me dead, as they all were threatening to do.

Then one day, who should come riding to the front gate but a strange gentleman in clerical attire. It was Father O'Toole who was in charge of the Roman Catholics of the parish. He told Ma that he would like to talk to that daughter of hers, if she did not object. Ma was hurt that a clergyman from another denomination should find it necessary to correct me, especially a Roman Catholic, as Catholics and Protestants have silly contentions concerning the copyright to heaven, but Ma is always a lady, so she invited Father O'Toole to come in.

Fortunately Pa had seen the arrival and came to my support. There was a great flow of geniality between them. Ma withdrew.

"Well, well, well," said Father O'Toole, laughing so heartily that I smiled. "Ye're a great girl and a right royal brave wan, but ye're all wrong on wan or two points that I'd like to indicate."

Here was a learned man of religious authority taking me seriously. I felt seasick. I just sat.

"Now, whoi on earth did ye set up to interfere with the birthrate?" He laughed again. "Arragh! Ye must have got ye'r ideas from that father of ye'rs."

Pa rubbed his hands together as he does when really pleased, and said I formulated my ideas myself; but he added that if a young person had a mind made for ideas they came out of the air.

I did not know what Father O'Toole meant by interference with the birthrate, but he said my condemnation of large families for pioneer women. Why, bless him, the country is crying out for population. Pioneering and population, according to him, are two things that should go together like strawberries and cream.

It was inspiriting to have a real person to argue with. I put forward my pity for overburdened women dying worn-out before their time. I advanced cases where even the doctors said the women would die if they had any more babies. "And what for?" I demanded. "Just to delve away from week to week at a lot of dull tasks — some of them superfluous. No beauty but the sunset and the moonlight."

His Reverence said that I was suffering from the divine discontent of genius, that it was a different matter with common people. If their noses weren't kept to the grind-

66

stone — Ha! Ha! Ha! — rearing families and working, they would get into all the devil's mischief in the world. Sure, we must fill up Australia and hold it from the Yellow Peril at our doors.

We must ourselves become a swarming menace to out-swarm the Yellow Peril! What a reason for spoiling our part of the earth! What a fate, to be driven to a competition in emulation of guinea pigs!

I pointed out to the Reverend gentleman that he didn't add to the population himself, that he was safe from the burdens of both fathers and mothers, that if he were a woman he might think differently. No woman should be expected to have a big family in addition to drudging at a dozen different trades. I suggested that the unfortunate Yellow Peril women might be relieved to enter into an alliance with us to stem the swarming business.

"Ah, but ye're all wrong, ye're arguing against NATURE. Ye mustn't interfere with Nature."

"As for that," interposed Pa, "All human civilization is a conquest of Nature."

"Yes, but ye can't change human nature." Father O'Toole laughed loudly.

"I don't think that to call an overdose of lust and verminous fecundity human nature is God's will," I contended, "and that I maintain, despite dads and the divils and all of divinity."

"Whoi would ye set yourself up against all of theology?"

"And why not? if her thinking apparatus suggested it," said Pa. "I often think myself that we have to take out a licence to keep a dog but the most undesirable man is not restricted in thrusting upon his fellows and his unfortunate wife, as many as a dozen repetitions of himself."

"Ah, 'tis only the old head talking through the young

67

voice," laughed Father O'Toole. "It's to be hoped she won't be brought into too much trouble. Och, ye're a fine girl, and a beauty to boot. The pity of it that ye're not a boy! Then we could make a priest of ye, and the many theological arguments and disquisitions we could have would put a different complexion on these things entirely."

Ma then brought in tea and the talk became ladylike and small. Our enlivening guest shook my hand kindly at parting as he said, "Ye can count me wan of ye'r friends and admirers though I think ye're wrong, young woman, but ye must grow to years of discretion."

Pa thanked him heartily for calling and invited him to come again which he promised to do, "To see what fresh mischief this young lady will be at."

"There's a man of the world," observed Pa, as he went. "I like him for coming openly as a friend, not a snake behind our backs."

"Huh!" said Ma. "He has the real old cackle like a political vote-catcher with his tongue in his cheek."

The following day I got a horrifying letter. The signature was bold and plain, so were the contents. It was from old Mr. Grayling who lived ten or fifteen miles away to the east. He was one of the most intimate of our friends. His wife had died about a year since. His daughters were Ma's great friends. He was seventy-two years of age — twenty-one years older than Pa.

I thought I was having a nightmare. It was a proposal of marriage. It sickened me to the core as something unclean.

Things were pretty bad for me, he said, when a blasted priest could think he had the right to denounce me, but that He (old Grayling) had faith in me. With his love and protection I could reinstate myself and be a very happy woman. He was a frantic Protestant and so set on his chart of the way to heaven that a cross drove him berserk as a symbol of popery rather than as the gallows on which Christ was crucified.

Old Grayling told me his age right out, but said he was younger at heart and otherwise than men half his age. Ugh! I cannot go on. UGH! UGH! UGH!

This was a desecration of all I had ever thought of love, of all the knights that were bold and heroes in lace and gold, and that sort of thing. Old Grayling was the most wrinkled man I know. He was stooped; he had only two or three barnacled fangs, and nothing gives a man such a mangy and impecunious appearance in the flesh as teeth like that. He had a BEARD. A straggly old-man one!

Petrified, sick, I hid behind the pig-sty for an hour or two. I had regarded him as a friendly grandfather. Why, he had three sons all with beards and bald heads and corporations! His granddaughters were older than I by years. It was as shocking as a case of indecent exposure against a bishop.

The pigs did not know what to think. They conversed to me and about me in the most friendly grunts. I love pigs. Observe how everyone cheers up at the mere mention or sight of pigs! In the animal kingdom one cannot ask for more engaging companions. They were my only refuge in that landscape. I couldn't even tell Pa this. It was too disgusting a revelation about another man so old. I tried to comfort myself by thinking Old Grayling must be suffering from delirium tremens, and this the equivalent of seeing snakes; but there wasn't really any comfort in it as I had never heard of his being drunk.

I tore the letter into bits and strewed it in the pigsty but every word was in my head. When I reappeared Ma asked me to explain my peculiar behaviour. I said I had been looking for the nest of a kangaroo rat. Ma said that was childish of me, but I got away with it because she was absorbed in Anthony Hordern's catalogue that the mail had brought.

Another sleepless and tortured night. I was in a sorry pass if clergymen of divers denominations could preach against me and call to admonish me so that Old Grayling could think himself a rescuer. My former state when I had chafed against monotony and lack of opportunity to try my wings with birds of my own feather now seemed deliciously peaceful. I had written a yarn just for fun, and every sort of person took it seriously and it collected duds and freaks upon me. Here was something like one of those murders or fires or other disasters that happen to strangers. Disgrace had rained upon me as suddenly as a thunderstorm.

I was abashed with one side of me but with the other I wished that Father O'Toole had proposed to me too. That would have been a situation to turn one camp a yellow tinged with green and give the other that pea-green feeling trimmed with orange, which would have been jolly good for both.

Chapter Eight.

More Chickens of Inexperience.

One day old Bismarck yelped and I looked out of the kitchen window to see Old Grayling approaching with a tall black blood which was being broken before my eyes on the bridle track between our place and one or two neighbours. A dry creek was almost impassable and mess-mate stumps were dotted thickly on either side of a narrow wriggling track. Along this came a man of 72 in a new single buggy — a show-ring affair — with a horse that leapt and sidled resentfully.

"Flash old fool!" remarked Pa. "He is bursting out again now that the old woman is underground."

"A wonder the family lets him run to such useless expense. He is mad to drive such a horse along that track," said Ma.

The Graylings were mortgaged through the front door and out the back gate. I knew why that odious old man had that horse and a new vehicle. He had eschewed riding but had come in competition with the young men who headed in my direction on Sundays and holidays leading race horses and other prime specimens wearing a lady's bridle. He had been a reckless young man. The district yielded yarns of his escapades. It was a feat, if I had not been so apprehensive of him, to see him bring that buggy and rampageous horse among the stumps and into that creek and up again at a dangerous angle and around our wood heap and over the garden drain to the side gate.

He was warmly welcomed by Pa and Ma. I kept near Ma while tea was being served. When Old Grayling began

71

to jockey me aside, I fled. He followed me to the garden, to the dairy, to the kitchen. I took the direction of a building to which no lady would be seen going. Desperation drove me to such a ruse. It was successful. The Graylings were renowned for gallantry.

I ran from there to the pigs again, risking the fleas for an unsuspected retreat. After a time Ma called. After some more time Pa hailed me with rousing coo-ees. The pigs talked to me but did not betray me. At length, peeping between the logs of the sty, I saw Mr. Grayling departing at racing speed guiding his intractable horse safely along the difficult track. I slid up the back way and into the kitchen. Ma and Pa, who had lingered watching the driving skill, were talking about me.

"She must be mad," it was Ma's voice. "To disappear without rhyme or reason."

"She shows no signs of madness," said Pa. "She might want to think."

At this I appeared. Ma demanded an explanation of my antics. I gave none.

"You make yourself very agreeable to the young men, but flout poor old Mr. Grayling. He waited till too late to drive home with that flighty horse just to say good-bye to you. Now is not the time to miss your manners if you want to live down the scandal and trouble you have caused."

Pa came with me to feed the pigs. "Your mother is right, you know, my girl. When we are kind to fine young men, it is not hospitality, it is self-indulgence. I always feel that any welcome I can give the Graylings is feeble compared with the welcome they give me."

The cause of my action seemed too indecent to tell Pa. As for telling Ma I would rather have had her report me to the doctor and clergyman as raving mad. She would blame me for Old Grayling's sickening aberration, and constant misunderstanding hurt. "Oh, Pa," I said, "I can't bear any more scandalmongering and fuss. I would as soon go and live with the pigs like the Prodigal Son."

This surprised Pa. He sat upon the pig-sty fence talking to me for a long time. "And you wanted to be famous," he said banteringly. "What you are undergoing is fame, the thing you wanted, in a very mild form."

"I didn't want bad notoriety: it must have been fair renown that I dreamed about."

"There is only one percent of that, mixed with exaggeration and scandal and envy. No one can make it otherwise, not even royalty, though it commands the press and the army. The smoking rooms are full of another story right around the world, always have been, even in days when one's head could be cut off for a disrespectful word about those in authority." Pa here quoted Byron.

"Why, my girl, it is wonderful at your age to be denounced by a preacher and argued with by a priest, though I can't see what the stir is about, myself. I'm sorry that you did not write something much more rousing. Surely you are man enough to stand up to a little flutter like this. Use common sense. Think what you say about other people. You don't like them any the less, but if they heard your private criticism of their clothes and persons there would'nt be a friend from Cape Otway to Cape Leeuwin. If you enter public life, you have to take all that as the chattering of magpies. As for people going to cut you dead, and that stuff that Eusty brings home; just walk out before them and smile, and they'll all be running to lick your boots and gain your favour."

Pa then went on to tell me of his experiences as a mem-

73

ber of the Legislature. "Bless me, I was accused of being a traitor to the State when I tried to bring in measures to help the under dog. I was called the misappropriator of funds for trying to save a great public swindle, and the fellows who carried it through were knighted."

Pa took me further into his confidence in a grown-up way.

"I was slandered — they even tried to defeat me by annoying your mother. They said she was a drunkard, which was madness, as you know."

Poor Ma, herself perfect and circumspect, first to have suffered the backwash from Pa's opponents and now to undergo a repetition through me! It made me understand Ma's attitude.

"You are old enough to face these things now," continued Pa and added in a whisper, "they even accused me of carrying on with other women."

This completely cheered me. I laughed until the pigs went whoof! whoof! whoof! all around the sty expecting a second helping. Pa and *other women!* was atrociously absurd, and Ma being accused of drunkenness was so abnormal that I was henceforward prepared for any stories about myself. Dear old Pa! Pa and OTHER WOMEN!

The prating about nothing new under the sun (Solomon) and the impossibility of upsetting antecedents, which met me when I wished to try something different, was gaining weight with me. Dismal. Now I could see why people have written those self-praising, white-washing autobiographies. People don't write autobiographies until they are old fogies. Otherwise they would have lacked time for EXPERIENCE, and EXPERIENCE had taught them before they started what it was teaching me now, that people can't endure their reality in print and so create an uncomfortable situation for the realistic autobiographer with his family and all concerned. Pa is always saying that when you get up in years you want peace, that it is only while you are very young or haven't any spiritual grist that you hanker for emotional tornadoes.

These lessons from Pa were a great help. Politics have seasoned him. He gives a whoof of contempt for gossip and scandal. He always turns what is said of him into a circus against the talebearer.

Things, all the same, are not simple. If I had stuck to my lords and ladies in England and a beautiful heroine who went through tophet to give the hero a chance to show-off as a deferred rescuer; if I had had the villain scrunching the gravel, and a jealous rival beauty biting her lips till the blood came and breaking the stem of a champagne glass between her jewelled fingers with rage (though I have not yet seen a champagne glass) I should have been acclaimed. My tale might have adorned the *Supplement to the Goulburn Evening Penny Post.* I love the tales in the *Penny Post,* full of mystery and glamour and castles and lords and gorgeous lovers. I don't know why on earth I became afflicted with this foolish notion of showing how comical the 'Possum Gully sort of reality would look by comparison. Aunt Jane is right, no doubt, when she says I was born contrary.

It was Old Harris who got me into this trouble by adjuring me to be Australian and thus add to culture. CULTURE! Talk about culture! ! ! I wrote to him on the subject.

There were fresh inconsistencies teasing me. Ma said that if I wasn't womanly and all that sort of triffle-traffle, the men would not propose to me, and here I was beset with proposals from all over the place. Some of

75

them were nearly as bad as Old Grayling's, though he was the dean of the faculty, but men cannot help nearly all being duds from the lover angle. I suppose their delirium of egotism keeps them perpendicular. I should never have the front to try to get a man to marry me, but you should see the objects that booby up to me and think they can have me for the asking.

There are others, always young and sometimes desirable who are so shy that I know them only in letters in which they confess they have followed me all day, recording my least action, or have sat on the same seat in Belmore Square and have heard the sound of my voice. There now!

One Sunday afternoon old Bismarck made an unusual commotion and called our attention to another exhibition of driving on the tortuous back track. A pair of spirited trotters swung around the stumps, down into the creek at a dizzy angle and up over the mere footbridge of the garden drain to fetch-up at the side gate. The turn-out was too good for a tea agent: it must be a wool agent. All kinds of agents are rather regarded as parasites upon the squatters and selectors — middlemen who fatten on the profits of commodities which other men sweat to produce. He looked like someone who had got out of his way and had called for directions. I hoped he was not coming in. I used to long for any sort of caller, but that infernal book has resulted in my being a kind of puppet show, and I am heartily sick of it.

Pa went out shouting surprise and a boomer of a welcome. Ma followed corroborating him, and asking the man why they had not seen him all these years. Pa and he went to the stables, leading the lovely ponies with their saucy heads and wide red nostrils. Ma hastened to spread a hearthrug and a table cover, kept for high company, and

76

said we'd have to prepare something for tea. We had tea on Sundays: other days Ma stuck to dinner at sundown instead of in the middle of the day. She was the only one in the neighborhood who did — a relic of her early social status.

It was Henry Beauchamp from Moongudgeonby, one of the big stations up the country, where Ma and Pa came from. He had been at their wedding and, since those days had been in Queensland and down the Murray. I did up my hair to look grown-up in readiness to meet him. Ma seemed delighted that he had come. As I came out he was saying she was the loveliest bride he had ever seen.

"Married life soon altered that," said Ma. "You haven't a bride of your own yet?"

"Can't find one to come up to you," said he. "Is your daughter like yourself?"

"Oh, dear me, no," said Ma expressively.

"Takes after you from what I hear," said Mr. Beauchamp, with a grin at Pa.

"They say so, but I think she is very much herself." I loved Pa for that and took this moment to come in.

The typical Australian squatter, according to my idea, rose to meet me. He was a tall broad man, with a clipped black beard and two or three grey hairs around the temples. Quite old. I noticed at once. He was so tanned that his eyes, a sort of oyster grey, looked like white holes. He smiled, showing white teeth, without waiting to be introduced. It was trying to have to come out in contrast to Ma, but I did not think I was grown-up enough for him to notice me much. I hoped he would not miss my complexion, which is one of my unassailable points. Everyone raves about it. My admirers always wish they could eat it. Ma says I get it from her as Pa's side have muddy

77

skins and that mine will soon go, that a complexion is a fleeting thing.

I think Henry Beauchamp noticed it and every other detail. His glances were quick and penetrating as if they could see through one's clothes.

There was a great flow of geniality and high company talk. Ma and Pa asked questions and Mr. Beauchamp replied in a soft cool voice. I liked looking at his teeth, but found his eyes on me wherever I went. This made me uneasy as I knew he was wondering how Ma, the perfect and unique, could have produced me. Pa and Ma had him in the evening while I did the work. I did not reappear until supper time at half past nine after which Ma showed Mr. Beauchamp to the spare room.

It was a wild windy night with tins rattling and rafters creaking and Pa hoped for rain, but the morning sky was bright and cold. At breakfast Ma suggested that Mr. Beauchamp should stay for the day. He accepted without quibble. He had had two big stages with his horses and a spell would do them good. They were a prize pair, had taken everything open to them at Bathurst, Junee, Cootamundra, Gool Gool and half a dozen other shows. He was to judge the horses at the Goulburn Show and had come a day or two in advance to visit Pa.

It was washing day and Ma and I wondered how he would put in the time. Moongudgeonby is a show place, and our cockatoo farm has nothing to exhibit. However, our guest seemed content to go about talking to Pa. They leant upon all the places possible and talked, even on the pigsty, while the pigs whoofed and seemed as pleased as they were to see me. They leant upon the sheep yards, and Ma said she would be ashamed for anyone who came from real sheep yards to see such makeshifts, but Mr.

Beauchamp did not criticise. They leaned against the stable door, and on the cow-yard fence and over the garden gate and talked and talked, and talked and talked.

Ma and I had to pull foot to get the washing out and the lunch on and look like ladies who had nothing to do. Pa was so pleased with a chum from his original grade that he invited Mr. Beauchamp to stay until the Show. He accepted without pressing. He did not seem to need exciting company. At lunch he said he would like one of the ladies to run into town with him next morning. Ma refused. He turned to me, but Pa said he would go, and it was a single-seated buggy. That settled that.

"Well then, I should like to take Miss Sybylla with me to the Show. A man by himself in a buggy looks forlorn, but Miss Sybylla would repair that."

I had promised to meet Billy Olliver but decided to ask him to let me off. He could come any day. This would be a thrilling jaunt with an escort so old and important. Twenty-six was the oldest I had yet, except Old Grayling. I went about my tasks like quicksilver hoping that Ruby and Nellie Blackshaw and the Crispin girls would see me driving with Mr. Beauchamp. They were going to look the other way when I came near. This would dish their airs.

The wind went out of my balloon while I was setting the table for dinner. Mr. Beauchamp was beside the fire while Ma was darning. It had come up cold. As I entered Ma was saying, "There seems to be no end to the annoyance caused by that silly book. I think it best to ignore all the scandal and it will die out. I assure you I knew nothing of it and have discouraged her all I can."

As I put the tray down Ma continued pointedly, "You asked if Sybylla resembled me. I should not like to think

79

so. She has given me a lot of vexation. I have had two mothers here bullying me because I have not restrained her from driving their sons mad. Men are foolish to think they can make any impression on her."

I felt myself reddening right through to my heels. Why will Ma hurt me so that I cannot sleep? She might have given me a chance with Mr. Beauchamp. I was being most circumspect. An older man like that, what would he think? I could not go to the Show with him after this.

I made faces at Ma and tried to stop her, and I think Mr. Beauchamp caught me, he was much amused, and led Ma on to say more.

"So Sybylla is a bit wild, is she? You must have spoilt her."

"She has spoilt herself. Men can't see that they might as well try to catch the wind or that old hawk out there, but they giggle-gaggle around her and overlook the nice quiet girls who would make men happy."

That was not fair of Ma. When I tried to escape Old Grayling, she said I was inhospitable. I treated everyone alike and they all admitted that I was friendly and full of fun.

I was so ashamed that I could not look Mr. Beauchamp in the eyes. I placed the lamp at his end of the table with a vase of flowers between me and him but he peeped around it and said I was getting lost so far away.

I disappeared to the kitchen for the evening to finish the ironing and to set bread. Ma was in the dining-room writing letters to send by the men in the morning. Mr. Blackshaw came over and he and Pa and Mr. Beauchamp were in the drawing-room or "front room" as the company room is called around 'Possum Gully.

Eusty had gone to bed and I had started on the ironing

when Mr. Beauchamp stood laughing at me from the doorway. I asked him if he wanted anything and he said, yes, a talk with me.

"I haven't time to talk," I said, fearing that Ma would blame me if she came out and found him there.

"Aren't you going to ask me to sit down?"

"I beg your pardon," I said, setting a stool before the fire. "I thought Pa would be wanting to talk to you."

I blithered away at the ironing. He placed the stool right before me.

"So you are a trouble to the lads of the district," he said with a chuckle and a soft pedal in his voice. "And your mother does not advertise you as a little dove."

I thumped like everything so that I couldn't hear him, but he cupped his hands like coo-eeing. I was afraid that I'd laugh, so saying that I had forgotten the bread, I dashed away and collected the tub, the yeast, the flour and potatoes and began setting the sponge.

"You are the quickest human being I ever saw," he remarked. "You are carrying on like this just because you are upset by what your mother was telling me."

"I'm not like what Ma says."

"Oh, ho, what about that book?"

"It's not real."

"I don't believe you are either. I have never seen any-one like you, and I've been about a bit in my time. I've had a bit too much time to be about in too," he added, and laughed so infectiously that I nearly joined in.

"In that case," said I, "you had better not waste any more time here."

"Oh, I don't grudge a little time to see if I can do anything to help my dear old friends with such a terrible daughter."

81

I worked furiously at the bread-setting.

"Well now, tell me about the book."

"I never talk about it. They all can think what they like. At least it has shown me how silly everyone is."

"I thought it had shown how silly you were. That's what I gathered from your cousins as I came along. They said it was the silliest goat of a book they ever read, and just what they expected as you are the silliest goat of a girl they have ever known."

I just stood and looked at him. I had not Pa's seasoning in meeting condemnation, especially from my cousins of whom I was so fond. At length I steadied enough to say, "At anyrate the greatest writer in Australia says I could be great some day if I develop."

"That poet fellow! Does his word count for anything? Writers are just skites, aren't they—half their time drunk and the rest of it cadging for a bit to eat?"

I was familiar with this point of view. All of my relations had it. None but Pa ever wrote so much as a letter to the newspapers, which put him among those sneered at as windbags trying to be important. I made the coffee and said, "You will be wanting your supper," and went to the dining-room.

Mr. Beauchamp went around the house and came in from the front pretending that he had been to the stables to let his horses out. Pa and Mr. Blackshaw were still talking. I went to bed, leaving Ma to dispense supper. Another tortured night. I was so fond of my cousins. I always defended them if anyone dared to say they were not the prettiest liveliest girls up the country.

Mr. Beauchamp and Pa left early in the morning and did not return until dinner time.

CHAPTER NINE.

IT WAS ALL REAL, BUT HOW MUCH WAS TRUE?

Mr. Beauchamp came straight to the kitchen after seeing about his horses.

"Last night you were quite put off your stride by what your mother and cousins think of you."

"If you don't mind, the subject is closed."

"Oh, no, it isn't," he said with his provokingly contagious laugh. "You were afraid it would affect my opinion of you."

"Your opinion . . . ."

"Now, now, don't try to break the bridle, or I'll tell your mother that you have been rude to me, and she won't permit that."

I devoted myself to the washing-up.

"I'll wait. You are so quick that you soon will be ready."

I turned my back on him.

"You have the prettiest neck and cheek from the back I ever saw," he remarked casually. "Don't be squiffy. I'll tell you something. Every word said against you weighs against those who say it. That sort of jealousy always works that way. All the girls from here to Timbuctoo are busy adoring you, and the one or two squeaks are pure jealousy."

"I never was jealous of anyone in my life."

"You have no one to be jealous of here. I wonder how you would shape among girls who could rival you."

83

This was a new point of view to me — an idea. I began to examine it and was trapped into talking.

"There are only two kinds of parents," he continued. "Those who think their offspring can do nothing wrong, and those who think they can do nothing right. My old man was in the same class as your mother. Every word of disparagement by your mother made me more interested in you. I would never think of marrying anything but a jolly little flirt. That kind of girl knows her way about, and you know when you have her. The booby might go off the rails at the least strain. Besides she has no fire or style."

"Yes, but I intend to be as annoying as I can in accordance with the family critics."

"Very clever of you: makes you provokingly attractive." He chortled again, "You are as full of mettle as a blood filly."

"I'll tell Ma that you are vulgar."

"She'd blame you. When she began to warn me against you, my interest was aroused. I know how to take the praise of fond mas with daughters on their hands. I'm not having any. There is no use in your playing up: the breed is there. Your father is the whitest man in Australia and any daughter reared by your mother is the real stuff, in a class by herself. There are a lot of old maids in your mother's family and that is another jolly good sign. Early marriage is often a sign of poor goods that have to be sold quickly."

Here was another idea. An interesting man.

"I'm glad you approve of old maids because I have decided to be one."

"But I shan't let you."

"What have you got to do with it?"

84

"Haven't you noticed my influence with your mother? Do you suppose I'm here to talk about the pigs and old times to your father: nearly staked my pair coming up that track."

"Aren't you married already?"

"No fear."

"Didn't sell early—are you good material?"

"Better call me Henry," he replied irrelevantly. "It will make me seem quite ten years younger."

"What for?"

"Well—you see—what age are you—eighteen?"

"Nearly."

"Whew! Only seventeen! You'll make a delightful little wife when the nonsense is trained out of you. Any man would want to marry you because of your mother."

"I don't know *your* mother, so I don't know if there is *any* reason at all why anyone would want to marry *you.*"

He laughed consumedly, I too; it was so silly.

"It is a serious consideration for a man of thirty-six to think of a girl of eighteen. Twenty years on I'll be an old chap wanting to settle down and you'll be just in your prime."

"Why consider such silly things without foundation?"

"Must I shave off my beard?"

"Why do you tolerate such a monstrosity?"

"It can go any minute you say."

"You might collapse like Samson and then need a winch to hoist you about."

"Do you like beards?"

"As if anyone could *like* a beard!"

"I must go to the barber tomorrow."

"Don't shave it off just yet."

"Why?"

"I shan't tell you." I had the laugh to myself now. After only thirty-five hours he seemed to be buckling like the young men, and what a trophy he would be, with his beard, like a big bear on a chain. This matter of beard was a lively test. I had applied it with the result that all my young men friends who had had moustaches were now clean-shaven, while those who had been clean-shaven were assiduously growing moustaches. Some of the latter were of the cricket style—eleven hairs a side.

"Well now, when I marry you I don't think I'll approve of any more of this writing. I'd be jealous of it. You'd want to be wasting your spare time on that when I wanted to play with you."

I flashed out at this. "Supposing I said that you would have to give up breeding wool or horses and be hanging around ready to play with me."

"That's a different matter. You're a woman, and Nature settled it long ago. I have nothing to do with it."

"But I have, you conceited lord of creation!"

At this Ma came in the door looking trenchantly at me. "Do you know that your daughter has just called me a conceited lord of creation?"

"Men deserve what they get for being so foolish," said Ma. "You are not going to be as silly as the boys, are you?"

I left him to Ma.

The following morning he again invited me to go to the Show with him in his buggy, drawn by the dashing pair that seemed to run above the road instead of on it. Ma and Pa both said I could go, Ma adding the rider, "If you behave yourself".

"I'll see that she behaves," said Mr. Beauchamp in his good-humoured drawl.

"And I'll see that he behaves," thinks I to myself, pricked to pay him out for his self-confidence. Billy Olliver was the instrument at hand. Billy's horse, Captain Phillip, was the best hunter of the year, and I had promised to take my habit and ride him in the lady's hack class. Well, my lord Henry could drive me to the door of the hotel, and when he came out I should be departing with Billy. There was time to send a letter and get the plot in train.

Then the Clerk of the Weather messed-up everything. We had suffered from a drought since Christmas, and it was now late in March. The sky was overcast. Henry received word to come in on the Wednesday for urgent business with the Show officials. He apologised, but said he would take charge of me the moment Pa and Ma arrived on Thursday morning, and would drive me to the Show Ground.

"Ha!" scoffed Ma. "You'll find you won't have your own way with a hard-shelled old lady-killer."

The drought took a notion to break on Wednesday. It poured all the afternoon so that I could hardly make old Bandicoot face it when I went to meet Great-aunt Jane, who was arriving from Gool Gool; and the cattle went shivering campwards with humped backs and lowered heads. It was called a heavy thunderstorm, most opportune to lay the dust for the morrow, but rain fell again during the night. The morning was grey, but held up sufficiently for us to start. I shared the back seat with Aunt Jane.

The rain got heavier and heavier, obscuring the horizon, and Auburn Street was running creeks as we took refuge in the hotel yard. Mr. Beauchamp and Billy were both at the front door awaiting us. They did not know each other, but had been talking.

The rain was so torrential that there was no hope of going to the Show Ground. Ring events were impossible until it lifted. When we came into the hotel parlour, Billy and Mr. Beauchamp were both there. I introduced them. Billy immediately "turned dawg" and looked most bilious.

Mr. Beauchamp was in high spirits. Something seemed to so amuse him that he could not contain himself. I whispered to him that my plans, like his, had to be altered somewhat, that I was to be photographed on Mr. Olliver's horse, but that Aunt Jane would companion him to the show. "She's a dear," I said. "Ma is never done singing her praises, and says she wishes I was only a quarter as good."

Mr. Beauchamp's eyes danced. I withdrew to Billy. He muttered a curse on the drought having taken this day to break and said that young Masters had a wonderful gramophone at the Royal and had invited me to come and hear it if the rain continued.

We set off at once, Billy carrying the handbag with my habit, as I could dress at the Royal later. I had friends there in mine host and his wards. Mr. Beauchamp came to the door and wished us well with unforced glee, but Billy looked angry and chapfallen.

"Is Beauchamp a married man?" he really hissed, as soon as we were safely in the street.

"No."

"What's he doing here?"

"He's the Show judge, and Ma and Pa knew him up the country."

88

"AAAAH! He told me he was staying at 'Possum Gully."

I wondered what Mr. Beauchamp could have said to Billy to make him so queer. He turned quite wooden. He had no reason to be glum, as I went off with him, keeping my word under Mr. Beauchamp's nose. Billy bought me the regulation chocolates—a huge box—and we proceeded to the gramophone until the clouds should break. One of the Masters from out our way was the proud possessor. It played "Arrah go on," and some other songs. During the recital a messenger arrived with a note for me.

Mr. Beauchamp wrote that my Great-aunt Jane showed the breed I came from. He had been going to tell my mother how I had deserted him, but he was so pleased with Auntie that he would let me off this time. It was signed *Harold Beecham.*

Billy growled, "It's from that mug with the beard I suppose."

Daddy Royal overheard him and chipped in, "Miss Sybylla would get a hundred notes if the young men knew where to find her. If I put a notice on my door that she needed someone to drive her home this evening, the police would have to regulate the rush. If not, the young men of the district would be decaying; and they have eaten too much bull beef for that."

Billy suggested we should go in a cab to see the pavilion exhibits. He was polite and thoughtful, helping me with my dress, and keeping the rain off me with a big new umbrella while we were getting in and out of the cab, but there was a sadness and quietness about him that I have not seen before. I hoped he was not catching a chill.

The rain kept on and on. There wasn't a hope of a

ring event, so we came back to the Royal. The messenger was waiting with another note Harold Beecham reported that he and Auntie were getting on splendidly. He hoped that I and young Olliver were enjoying ourselves only half as much. If there was anything I would like him to do for me I had only to let him know. The postscript ran, "Ask young Olliver if he will grow a beard for you."

The messenger said he had to wait for a reply. I was delighted to oblige: "Yes, there is something you can do, thank you very much. Propose to dear Aunt Jane. I should adore you for an uncle, and it is a pity to waste such an avuncular beard."

I was pleased with the opportunity to use the word *avuncular*.

"Would you grow a beard for anyone you liked?" I asked Billy Olliver.

"I know what put that into your head," he snorted, and fell into a deep gloom.

Daddy Royal invited me to lunch and put me on his right hand side and kept up a patter of teasing. Billy sat on the other side of me and had rather a bad time. He seemed unfledged in meeting it after Henry Beauchamp. Tame. The subject of beards came up among the girls of the house, and some wag asked Mine Host if he thought a man ought to grow a beard to please a lady.

"Of course he should. I'm a Methuselah and have a beard already, but if I had the honour, now, say, of escorting Miss Sybylla for a day, I'd grow my hair and train it in a peruke. Billy Olliver, give an account of yourself. Why have you the privilege of sitting where you sit today, when all the upstanding young men of the district would eat their hats to be where you are at this moment?"

90

Poor Billy looked worse and worse. I tried to comfort him, but was puzzled by his behaviour. Perhaps he was a philanthropist and liked me while convention was against me, but hadn't the know-how to act up to the situation which had suddenly overtaken us.

Another note arrived at the end of lunch.

"Your mischief is like a tonic. Never enjoyed myself more. Your father has invited me to spend a week with him after the Show, and then I'll get my innings. I bet young Olliver's cake is turning to dough already. Let me know your thoughts by the messenger."

I wrote: "My thought is that you are very silly. Don't blame me. I haven't said a word, but everyone in town will know that the messenger is from you."

The messenger was back in twenty minutes: "It's downright unkind of you not to mention me. What do you suppose I'm sending a man back and forth for but to keep myself to the front. If my only object was to employ a messenger I could give him five bob and let him rest his corns."

Billy growled, "You must be very spoony if you have to write to him every two minutes."

Mr. Beauchamp had me on tip-toe to play ball with him, but I could not make him angry. He laughed with imperturbable good humour.

The rain never let-up for a moment. Everyone settled down to a comfortable day indoors. We had a jolly time at the Royal with flirtation and chocolates, badinage and so on, mingled in equal parts. The prospects of grass for the winter cheered everyone.

"The rain'll do more good than the Show," the publicans said, as they reaped an advance harvest.

As the afternoon deepened the messenger represented Pa, and I had to return to the Commercial. It was too wet to ride home with Billy, as we had intended, so I tucked in beside Aunt Jane.

Billy escorted me to the last and said good-bye with chocolates, the only backsheesh I was permitted to collect from admirers.

It was a long wet drive. In spite of macintoshes, umbrellas and rugs, the rain drove through cracks, and we reached home cold and damp. Eusty had a roaring fire and the tea set, and soon we were all comfortable around it, talking over the day.

"Dear me, what an interesting man Mr. Beauchamp has developed into," remarked Aunt Jane. "Most of the young men are interesting until they begin to cackle with Sybylla and turn into perfect idiots." Aunt Jane was disapproving of my disappearance all day, but Pa said I was as safe as in a church at the Royal.

I had received a letter from Old Harris in reply to my complaints of my woes. The sympathy in it rose to understanding and was as liberating as a new idea.

He stated that fowls would always peck at the wild swan that was hatched among them until it grew strong enough to escape. As to the excessive number of people who claimed that they had been caricatured, the more of these the greater the tribute to my gifts of characterisation: it was valuable evidence which should elate rather than depress. He went on to say that one should be magnanimous about misplaced censure as the day was swiftly coming when it would be reversed. The future boast of my associates would be that they had known me. He implored me to remember that I wore the mantle of genius—a royal mantle which should never be lined with rancour. He said he hoped to see me in London whither he was soon returning. I would find my rightful place there. I was as out of my element in 'Possum Gully as a swan in the Sahara. "Your wings, my brave girl," he concluded, "are fashioned for grand flight. Lift them up and soar, and if an old man who once knew the world overseas, to which you will soon gravitate, may venture a word of advice: think and wait, make no entanglements to cripple the power of long distance flight."

He enclosed some English reviews. One of two columns in length compared my gifts with those of several immortals. The printed word was irrefutable, though I could not show the reviews abroad or I should be accused of blowing my own horn.

It was a stimulating letter. I brought it to Pa in triumph. It had been quite a heady day. Pa was more excited than I. "I knew, my girl! I knew!"

It seemed as if 'Possum Gully might not have the last word about me. Aunt Jane had that: "It sounds as if poor Old Harris must be drinking more than ever."

My balloon was pricked. Bang! BUNG! it went.

CHAPTER TEN.

HAROLD BEECHAM AND FIVE-BOB DOWNS.

"Harold" came out as he threatened after the Show, and quite settled down with us. My elders talked about him and stopped when I came near. It made the housework quite entertaining to receive a note every half hour or so. I got into the habit of replying. First I put on his table the long English review; then a whole page one from the philosopher of the *Squatters' Journal.*

"I don't know about this English Johnnie," he said, "but old Frogabollow in the Journal, I always wonder why they let him have so much space when it could be given to the latest prices. I must see what he says."

This was daunting, so my next shot was the letter from the GREATEST AUSTRALIAN WRITER.

"I always thought that booze and rattiness and 'pomes' went together," was the response to this. "So I must get your blooming little book and see what it is all about."

"Haven't you read it?"

"Never read a book since I left school. I had a cook last year who used to sit and read penny dreadfuls till the bread rose over the tub and fell on the floor."

I did not know how to cope with this. I fell into a Government Dam of silence. Books were an excitement and joy to me. In teaching me manners Ma had laid down the rule, "When you don't know what to say, say nothing." I said nothing. I went on with my housework.

94

I shuddered. If I missed a stroke anywhere it would be put down to my inclination to write. Other girls could border on being slatterns without attracting attention.

I suddenly felt unhappy and full of failure.

No one that I knew had ever seen a real live author. I had imagined them as having different qualities of soul and intellect. When I had found myself in print—a suffering, mistake-making, walk-about person—it resulted in a frightful drop in the stock of authors. I had thought critics to be above authors as school teachers are above scholars. This English one must have been drunk—like Old Harris. The contemptuous dismissal of his praise was supported by Mr. Beauchamp's attitude, and at times men who worked on the *Penny Post* had stayed with us, and there were tales that they could have been on big Sydney papers but for drink.

"Do you think I should read your book?" Mr. Beauchamp asked later.

"I wish you would never read it, but I can't make out why you are interested in me, if you haven't."

"All the hubbub has brought you to my attention, like a filly that is advertised. I could not make out why Moongudgeonby was suddenly being called Five-Bob Downs, and found that it was because in a book written by some bit of a kid no bigger than a bee's knee, Five-Bob Downs was owned by Harold Beecham, so people have the cheek to call me that. Some of them have asked me when I am going to settle down with Sybylla Melvyn. The young fellows say I am a lucky devil, that they would have a shot for themselves only that I am the hero of your dreams. I took it as a bit of chyacking while I was in Queensland, but when I got back to Gool Gool people buzzed like a swarm of bees. I thought it a

95

rum thing that a girl could change the name of a place christened by the blacks hundreds of years ago. She must be a witch who could pull the wool over my eyes and have me tied up before I knew where I was, and I value my freedom."

I began to feel worse than when Old Grayling's letter came.

"I never thought of you—never heard of you," I gasped weakly.

"But Harold Beecham is the fellow that all the girls are wild to see, and all the men are envious of."

"But your name is Henry Beauchamp," I murmured, wishing I could hide for a year.

"But I was nearly christened Harold, and Beauchamp is pronounced Beecham."

"Harold is my favourite name—Harold Earl of Kent, who fell at the Battle of Hastings with an arrow through his eye. A tragic thing to be conquered by an outsider. You have not the slightest resemblance to the Harold in the book. The name is a mere coincidence." My voice would hardly come.

"Ha! Ha! A jolly coincidence. I know half-a-dozen young fellows who are pretending they are Harold Beecham without the name. When I found out you were Dick Melvyn's youngster I was more astonished than ever, and came along to take a look at you. As soon as I clapped an eye on you I decided that I was going to take up my option."

"What option?"

"On you. You proposed to me. I accept with alacrity. I would not have thought an oldster like me had a chance, only you put it in my head. I always go for first-class things and leave the ordinary stuff to the rabble."

96

All the shame I had hitherto felt rolled into one lump was an infant to what I felt now. I, who would rather have died than "throw myself at a man", seemingly had done just that. Ma was quite correct. There was no end to the annoyance caused by that feraboraceous book. I turned sick all through to think what further embroglios might spring from it. More and more I understood Ma, and was sorry for what I had brought upon her.

"Please understand," I pled. "I never thought of you. The book is not real. The girl is only make-believe, and Harold Beecham a figment of imagination."

"That's what is so nice," he laughed. "Make-believe and life are sometimes the same thing. You are Sybylla Melvyn, I am Harold Beecham, and not going to relinquish my advantage."

What was I to do? I had a wild desire for flight, but he slipped into the doorway and was too big for me to pass. Was there anyone in all the world who would understand the mess I was in, or my agony of sensitiveness? I jammed my lips together to keep them steady, and sat down despairingly. Oh, why didn't he understand; and how I could have adored him if he had!

"I'd like to put you in my waistcoat pocket and keep you safe," he said, not laughing any more. "It suits me all to pieces to get into the show. I can give you so many things that you'll soon forget you ever wrote a book."

"Please go away where you won't see me any more," I said. "I am terribly upset by what has happened. Goodnight!"

He did not try to detain me. I went to my room. He slipped a note under my door before he went to bed: "The only thing doubtful is my age, otherwise you have made me the proudest man in Australia."

I lay awake all night shivering with distress and listening to the mopokes and willy wagtails. A strayed cow was as sleepless as myself, and told the world. A piffling wind sucked the blind against the window panes and teetered in the leaves of the trees. Pa snored and was chid by Ma. All these sounds measured the silence of the night which at length was terminated by the waking poultry, and I had to face the day and Harold Beecham. Fortunately he departed early to inspect stock, as he had grass to spare. On other days he attended the sales in Goulburn, which is a big centre. He returned incredible distances to spend the nights at 'Possum Gully. The surplus condition was knocked off those flying ponies.

Grandma took a hand presently. Possibly Aunt Jane had reported, though Aunt Jane was jolly good for an old codger, and carried on her combats with me single-handed without tittle-tatting. Grandma seemed to stamp over Ma and be as contemptuous of her as Ma is of me. It was disgraceful, she said, for a girl to be so much talked about as Sybylla was. What on earth could Ma be doing to allow it? She did not like to hear of me attracting Henry Beauchamp, a dirty old fellow who could cast his eye on married women, and who should have had a wife of his own long ago, seeing he had plenty to keep one.

Bang, bang, went romance under Grandma's touch!

She could not sleep at night for fear she would hear of me coming to harm. I was sick of this "coming to harm" notion. According to it girls have always to be chaperoned or armed against men's ravening. My experience so far has contained no hint of such unbuttonedness. Not one of my lovers ever put his hand on me except to my toe to toss me to horse back. As for a kiss, I should have fled in horror from one so unchaste as to

98

suggest such a thing. In my code, a kiss could come only after definite engagement. Pa always said, "It doesn't matter what a man says to you: words cannot hurt us if we have sense, but never allow a man to place his hand on you. Make him show his respect by keeping his distance."

The men evidently knew this as well as Pa, and acted upon it scrupulously. They never disrespected me further than to beg me to marry them. Some of them offered in return to leave Australia to settle in South Africa or New Zealand to meet my desire for travel. City people, of course, were much more wicked than country ones. It is probably city men, I thought, who are sensual and coarse.

Grandma's suspicions roused even Ma's dander a little. She said as a girl it had always been annoying to her to be watched as if she were an incontinent drab who couldn't impose respect upon any man she ever met. During this attack of Grannie's, Ma was the least off my side I had ever known her. She said, however, if I intended to marry, I had better think of picking the best of the men who came along, as Pa was useless as a provider, and in a world arranged as this one was, the only boat to success for a woman is a rich man to dote on her and back her up. It was all very fine while I was young and saucy to be giggle-gaggling, but I would early find that a girl had small choice. It would be a miracle if there was someone at all acceptable. That is how Ma had found it.

Ma was not at all a slavish advocate of marriage. She said if women had the sense to organise themselves and refrain from marriage till they had won better conditions there wouldn't be so many wives wishing they had had some other chance to earn their living, nor so many spinsters either thankful they had escaped marriage or

99

regretful that they had not known the fulfilment of love. Ma said also that many girls married out of mere curiosity, but quickly had too much of THAT.

Grandma wrote again that if Beauchamp was in earnest it would be a lucky disposal of me, Richard being such a failure and I so self-willed. Grandma was away back in the stages of thinking that it was natural for women to be quelled by marriage and the giving birth to as many children as God's will or a rabbit's example dictated. She and Father O'Toole were in the same boat in putting God's will and the rabbit's instinct on the one level, though Grannie was such a vigorous Protestant and Father O'Toole such a sealed Roman that either would have argued till he or she was blue without budging an inch, and have called the other a benighted bigot.

Aren't old people silly when you question their ideas, and yet they prate at us as if they were God Himself!

The bickering continued about me and Henry and other young men. When I came to think it over, I never heard Grannie say a good word of Ma, and yet Ma was the most beautiful and capable daughter a woman could have. Ma was passing on this piece of heredity. Perhaps, I began to think, you could not respect a thing you made yourself, or else they had such high standards that they concentrated on flaws and took excellences for granted. There were other mothers though who thought their children marvels because they were their own.

Grandma wanted to know had Beauchamp taken up permanent residence with us. If he was trifling with me, it was in rather a queer way. I had a hundred notes, most of them telling me what he was going to do with me when he married me. And he had had a long talk with Pa, who said not to worry me yet. I said I would not think of marrying until I was at least forty. Henry said no one would want to marry me then, and I said I would not want them to, so we would be quits.

He would laugh with unruffled good-humour. "You're as good as Mrs. Henry Beauchamp already. You cooked your own fish. I'm ready to spell my name Beecham to fit in—more sensible in any case. I'm willing to wait a year."

I said I would not marry Adonis himself, until I was twenty-one, and he said he would wait three years, but not another day. I murmured that sixty would be early enough to enter the field of bad health for women called marriage.

"What whims you have. Marriage is a sacred institution."

"That's superstition you have foisted on to us just to clamp us down for your own amusement."

However, upon finding that he and his station were connected with my book I felt responsible. This put much worry into my soul and took the fun out of parrying his advances. How I longed for someone to understand and help me. Old Harris might have understood well enough to decide if I must in honour submit to this "entanglement", but he had gone to England and had not yet sent me his address. I played for time.

Into these days of surface entertainment and underground worry Old Grayling again barged like a mad bull. He was just as luny as our most aristocratic bull, who would put himself against fence posts or toss gates on his horns and tear up anything that came in his way, even his favourite heifers. At certain seasons we had to leave everything open until he calmed down.

Old Grayling came jolting and swaying up to the side

101

gate, the black now considerably subdued, but incited to
show off, as the flash young shearer pricks up his horse
when he thinks the girls are looking. Pa and Henry went
out to meet him. Grayling gave the reins to Pa and
roared, "I have come to see Sybylla. She avoids me. She
does not answer my letters. I make her an honourable
proposal of marriage. I'm prepared to give way to her
in everything . . . "

I fled. Old Grayling caught sight of my dress as I
dashed in the front gate and along the verandah to the
spare bedroom. With a shout and surprising speed he
leapt after me. He looked in the door, but I was under
the bed, and he dived into the main house. I scrambled
out the window, scattering Henry's brushes as I went.
Old Grayling caught another glimpse of me from the
back door. Pa was left in bewilderment with the horse.

The old toad suspected me of a repetition of tactics
and tore to an unmentionable apartment to outwit me.
I saw him leathering past from the shelter of the fowl
house and sped once more to the consoling friendliness
of the pigs. A motherly old sow enjoyed being scratched,
and stood contentedly as a screen while I indulged her.

I could descry unusual motion at the house. Ma came
out and about looking for me. Aunt Jane followed, then
Pa and Henry. They had a colloquy, after which Pa
went to the outhouse, knocked on the door and asked Mr.
Grayling if he were ill. He came out and began to rage.
I could not hear it all because I had to huddle behind the
sow. She thought I wanted a drink, and grunted so loudly
that much of the argument was lost; also they went behind the fowl houses and that cut off their voices.

Ma came to the gate and called that tea was ready, and
I saw Pa urging Old Grayling to come. He waved his

arms like a wind mill and bellowed a little, but soon they went inside together.

Henry came from the kitchen calling softly to me and looking everywhere and saying, "I know where you are." Now and again he laughed to himself till he shook, which showed that he had no understanding of my feelings. It was coarse and thick-skinned to laugh at such a caricature of LOVE, when he himself was pretending to be in its thrall.

After a while Pa came looking for him, and when they disappeared inside, I said ta-ta to the pigs. Feeding time was approaching, and I meant to stay out all night or until Old Grayling left. I circled to the hayshed where I climbed near the roof and made a warm sweet-smelling nest. Baby mice squeaked, and a lizard visited me, and I must have been there two hours when Pa came for the horse. Old Grayling shook hands all round and drove away at a wild bat. I slid down, took every straw off me, crept around by the buggy shed and sheep yards, and reappeared as if I had come over the hill. Pa was feeding the pigs, who were squealing at being neglected, and he came to meet me.

Pa never said a flaying word to me in his life, no matter how debbil-debbil I may have been. "I'm sorry you have been frightened, my girl," he said.

I wasn't frightened. Thunderstorms, mad swaggies, bulls breaking out, fractious horses, bush fires—any of the things that frighten most girls—do not upset me, but things about which they exchange smutty confidences can sicken me all through and drop me in a cauldron of nerves. This was one of them.

Pa inquired how it had begun. I told him of the letter

103

and how I had run away before and how Ma had scolded me for being remiss.

"But we never suspected. If you had confided in your mother all this could have been avoided."

"Oh," I said, shrivelling, "it has disgusted me so that I'd hate Ma to say the wrong thing."

"Your mother is a wonderful woman. I'll speak to her. You'll have to be wise and full of mercy in meeting all these situations."

Aunt Jane was a boon as she kept Henry talking in the front garden while I plunged into preparations for dinner. Pa moved in and out of the kitchen bringing wood and filling the water cask, as a protection. During dinner I kept behind the flowers, and Henry never said a word to me, though I knew that his eyes were constantly on me.

Afterwards Ma helped me wash-up and sent Eusty to turn the horses out.

"You should have told me when Mr. Grayling first wrote to you," she said, but not in a disciplinary tone.

"Oh, I couldn't! You always blame me so, and I could not stand any more. Loathsome old toad, he makes me sick." I burst into tears and hid in the pantry and left Ma to the work. She did it like a lamb.

"Come," she said at length, "no harm has been done. The poor old man is childish, and this has overtaken him. Old men are often like that."

"Do old women go like that too?" I asked, overcome by a horrifying possibility.

"No. Old women are never as silly as old men. When he comes again, go into my room and I'll say you are not here for the day; and he will soon be himself again."

Ma had never been so clement to me. She further acquiesced that I should retire without reappearing. As

I lay awake I pondered another inconsistency. If old men being thus disgusting was so usual that Ma could be quite calm about it, why did men give themselves such airs about having all the brains and strength of mind? The more I thought, the more did old men seem like the God they had set up in their own image for women and children to worship.

Chapter Eleven.

Not So Expurgated.

Life is not all as black as ink, even in an unliterary
career. After Pa and Ma came to my help concerning
Old Grayling, things took on a different aspect.

Henry went away for the winter to look after property in Queensland. I did not agree to be definitely
engaged, but could not be hoity-toity seeing how I had
implicated him in my misadventure. I was in hopes that
he would tire of me before long. He was content to
wait for three years. He said it would be safer if I
looked around to see if I found anyone that I could like
better than myself. If I did not he was sure that I would
not find anyone whom I liked better than *himself.* "I
don't want you to buy a pig in a poke," he said and
laughed. It was nice of him to ease up on the Harold
Beecham and Five-Bob Downs embarrassment.

As I would not break my training and accept a present,
he got around the rules by leaving me a dashing filly to
ride, called Popinjay. He also gave me a diary as a keep-
sake, in which I was to write a list of those I met and
everything I thought, to read to him when next we met.

Tell him all I thought! Well, what do you think?

More and more English criticisms arrived and frightened
me by their approbation. A Melbourne editor printed ex-
tracts from the whole tribe to controvert those who held
that I should have been whipped for writing such a bad
advertisement of Australians and shut up in a strict school

until I outgrew my misguidedness. Ma kept the paper on the sitting-room table, where it could be seen. Some of the critics compared me to Emily Brontë. Zola and Dickens were other names used in comparison. The more high-flown a critic the more cordially he welcomed me as an audacious child who spoke unaffectedly from the heart.

Paradoxically, it was the people who knew my types by heart who reviled me as a liar and hypocrite. Dear old fellow-residents of Wallaby Range, I can see after these scarifying years the pathos of their disapproval, when for the first time they saw their own reality in print. No doubt they longed for something of the beauty of life, even as I, though in a less passionate and rebellious degree: or they may have imagined that in fiction they would be transmogrified into cavaliers like those in the stories in the *Penny Post*. It was too dismantling to find themselves in their own old beards and coats, and conversations about the crops and droughts and pudding recipes and little Tommies' toe aches.

Nevertheless there was a new tide of complaints from those who blamed me for neglecting them. A curate lectured me as an ignoramus that I did not include him—an Oxford University graduate. I had missed my only chance to portray culture. Lordy, had I thought of doing him, he might have been punctured by my view of his stuffed magpie education and the Oxford impediment in his speech.

Other emissaries of the church came to denounce me to my face. Tales of those who tiraded behind my back were frequent—whether church wardens, local preachers, precentors, acolytes or other scribes and pharisees soon became a jumbled mass. We parted in a spirit of mutual unvanquishedness. They had every established institution

107

on their side in one way or another, dependent upon whether they followed the Protestant or Roman Catholic recipe for endowing God with undesirable qualities, but I had Pa on my side and he assured me that TIME also was with me.

One gentle old Canon so impressed me that I thought him quite a gun. He was as thin as a lath which was appealing because the tickling Canon was balloony. This dear soul said when young himself, he had suffered torturing doubt and lonely seeking similar to mine. Patience and experience (how I hate patience, and there was Ma's panacea—EXPERIENCE!) would garden my soul and show the futility of seeking peace in extraneous things. We must cleanse our hearts and look within for truth and salvation.

I abhorred the deadliness of peace, and was hankering for joy. The Salvation Army thumping tin cans and wearing ugly bonnets and roaring about being saved in such an unladylike way had too much of a corner on salvation to leave it any glamour.

One of the last to appear was the tickling Canon. Ma welcomed him and handed him the Melbourne paper, remarking that he might be interested to see what interest was taken in her daughter in England. Ma said she was surprised that he had been so dilatory—*dilatory* mind you, but Ma is no vassal—in coming to see Sybylla. No wonder the church was losing its influence when a young girl had to depend on the sympathy of other pastors than her own. She neatly mentioned the names of Father O'Toole and other educated odds and ends. I withdrew so as not to explode with pleased surprise. Fancy Ma!

The Canon was not at all haw-haw when I came in again. Softened by Ma's support, I sat as demurely as a mopoke. He congratulated me. I thanked him. After a while he recovered slightly and said, "You can't expect me to agree with you *in toto*." (I could not find this in the dictionary, but it sounded like Trilby's "altogether" in ideas.) Ma invited the Canon to lunch, but he had promised to return to the Ollivers. Selah!

Other callers were tanned men all the way from the Cooper or the Paroo to bring me souvenirs or to shake the hand that had penned the book. Others wrote from Riverina and Out Back that they had met a man who had seen me. There were many whom I had never seen who gained notice by meeting me in places I had never been. Many others claimed relationship which did not exist. I was for ever hearing of cousins from Cape York to the Leeuwin—cousins in their own imagination. My real cousins, with a few exceptions, from Cape Otway to Charters Towers, maintained social superiority by deploring me as unworthy of the family progeniture. Inconsistently the people who had intended to turn their backs on me to illustrate my inferiority now reversed to attest their equality. The girls now said they did not mind how high I went, because I was not conceited and had never put on the slightest side. Pa, through EXPERIENCE, had predicted this.

The queerest characters thought they were my twin souls, and without having read my book. A far-flung tribulation of girls claimed me as their other self. People not near enough to feel caricatured loved my outburst because it was "just like ourselves". They thanked me for my pluck and ability. I had given them all a lead in letting-go in egotism, and they found it a boon. My shrieks of discontent necessarily being crude and unformulated, and my fellows of all ages and no attainments, so to speak, also being crude and unformulated, or having been crude and young and unformulated, found me an affinity. Egotism can conceive no higher compliment.

And all is egotism. The only people whose mainspring is not egotism are the dead, and perhaps idiots—the one class having ceased to have a main-spring and it having been omitted from the works of the others. Immediately people's egotism fails them, if they are not on the point of death from senile decay, they commit suicide. Egotism is the spirit of self which is designated human nature. The more human nature one has, the more egotism. Some people are not so readily fitted with the adjective of egotistical as others because they are not such pronounced types or are cunning in dissimulation. There are of course different brands of egotism. Some egotists are lovable and some not. The child is the perfect example of egotism, and the most lovable. One of the lovable kinds among adults is he with a high sensitiveness which can be used as a thermometer to gauge the worries and desires of his fellows' heads and hearts. Such are classified as sympathetic. The commonest, the least interesting, have their egotism interwoven with a delusion that their most banal experiences are unique. These are called bores. The intense egotism of another class is so charming that it is called personality, but all human manifestations are brewed from egotism—it is their major psychological content.

Leading people, some of them set aloft by money, hired vehicles in Goulburn and harried their horses in getting lost among the stumps of back tracks and bridle tracks, and found their way to call on us. One was an old gentleman of individuality in the matter of grey toppers and leggings. He paid an investigatory visit to Pa on behalf of his brother philosophers, or windbags as they would have been called only they had money too. Pa and he had a long, mysterious conversation out near the beehives and quince trees.

Pa told us about it afterwards. Grey Topper wanted to know unmentionable and intimate things about my prenatal days. The Governor-General, who had literary leanings, was responsible for classifying me as a genius, so a genius I became. Grey Topper and his coterie had a theory that a genius arrived from a mother who had far from enjoyed surrendering to a satyr.

I knew of a satyr as the mythological beast. To apply this to Pa was productive of chortles. The dictionary divulged the word's fissiparations: "A very lecherous person and a species of butterfly."

Pa did not fit any of these. When other women were divulging the atrocities which appear to be a normal risk of marriage, Ma would always say, "Thank God, I have never had to endure anything like that." Ma would add that any woman who did, deserved it.

Ma disdained Grey Topper's theory, though her remarks confirmed rather than exploded it. She said she never seemed to come to the end of the foolishness of men, this à propos Grey Topper having time as well as the indelicacy to trot about prying into such matters. Ma added that it was only men's maniacal egotism and complacency that enabled them to wreak their will regardless of women's revulsion and weariness.

Ma seemed all right in her half of the recipe for genius. It must have been dear old Pa who had failed in the satyr business.

Old Grayling was unregenerate and his senility was incurable, so Pa and Ma decided to accept one of the many

111

invitations that came for me at that time. Mrs. P. Darius Crasterton was most pressing. The Rt. Hon. P. Darius had been Minister for Lands when Pa had been member for Gool Gool. His widow assured Ma that she would chaperone me carefully and that I should see all the best people—the worth-while ones of weight in the country.

Pa recalled that the old man had made his fortune by rake-offs in the distribution of railway lines during his administration. Pa had lost his seat because he had resisted the swindle of taking the railway around by some big fellows' runs instead of through a farming district. Old Crasterton and one Sir James Hobnob later had had their way and grew rich and honoured, while Pa became poor and obscure. Pa said he did not suppose that the old woman could help her husband's misappropriation of public funds: I could see the world with her and learn to judge it.

What I would be able to pick up from people who "really mattered", she said, would be an invaluable education to me with my "very considerable but uncultivated natural gifts", and that what counted in cultivating good style were the "contacts" which she would be able to give me.

She mispelled *litreature, privilidge* and *realy,* but not to spell correctly is sometimes considered a sign of genius and sometimes a lack of education. The thing was to find out when it was which. Ma had a struggle to find the railway fare, but there was a cheap excursion, and Mrs. Crasterton said she would be pleased to give me some dresses in return for the pleasure it would be to have my fresh young company.

Ma warned me against putting myself under obligations. "You'll be more self-respecting if you don't," said she.

Pa said "Hoh! the people who want you for your clothes are not worth knowing."

"Nevertheless, I can't send the child away naked," said Ma.

I craved a long dress, but Ma said that would involve more than she could afford. If I kept my hair down I was still a girl "not out", staying with Mrs. Crasterton, and it would be simpler for everyone. She made me a dress of white organdie. It had frills at the cuffs and two flounces, and tucks all over the bodice. Ma could sew better than anyone else, and cut out with a beautiful line. The dress was finished with a bow at the V of the sailor collar, and I had more ribbon to tie my pigtail in a bump on my neck, something like the bob-tailed draught horses at the Show. I longed for a blue sash, but Ma said it would be useless expense and that only tall slender girls could wear sashes.

What did it matter about a sash when I was on the way to the station to go to Sydney, a cauldron of excitement about the holiday that was coming—my first visit to the city! I also dwelt upon the aristocratic address to which I was bound.

Chapter Twelve.

The Denizens of Geebung Villa.

Goulburn slid behind. I felt all crumbly and full of pangs that poor old Pa and Ma were not coming too, but they both had been to Sydney often in days gone by. I was bubbling with glee inside like a bottle of honey-mead. If the stopper had not been firmly tied I'd have effervesced right out in one high jet.

There was nothing joyful in the landscape. It was naturally barren and scraggly and dry, and now dotted with dead beasts. Those alive were so pitifully frail that it was painful to behold them. Milch cows being beaten in and out of bails and dusty yards, in such condition, was surely a cruel purgatory for animals. But the coastal belt approached with everything green and soft, and ferns and shrubs and flowers not to be seen inland. I ran out on the platform at each stop to see all I could. Liverpool, and after that it all seemed town. Strathfield and the roar of the city like a flood. Surging, exciting. It gave me tremors all over. The racket of the trains passing each other shocked like blows. Sydney was all around me. I was swamped by new feelings.

I was to be the guest of people who were somebody, I was to see all the sights and meet heaps and heaps of people, and work at nothing but pleasure from morning till night for a month!

I stood beside Pa's old Gladstone bag—my only luggage—and when most of the passengers had gone a large old lady came and claimed me with: "This is my little girl, I know. I am Mrs. Crasterton." She gave me a friendly kiss and said, "This is my brother."

A man much her own general cut but younger, greeted me with a chummy nod and a flabby handshake. Mrs. Crasterton was weirdly smart. She had "kept her figure" with corset and belts as strong as patent wire strainers. The brother had a short figure, enlarged by a corpulency. He was instantly ruled out as an object of romance. Knights of the imagination are straight and slim, preferably tall and beautiful. Married men, however, have a false importance through their wives that one has to recognise; and in most cases it is impossible to conceive what elderly people ever saw in each other to admire.

I put the brother in the married class. He took a side-long squint at me like a judicial old cockatoo. His sister called him Gaddie, but he did not look it. He carried my port along the platform and put Mrs. Crasterton and me in a cab and muttered, "See you later."

The first thing I noticed about Sydney streets was the rain rushing through them in muddy torrents and a tram with water spraying out of its rear to the derision of the bystanders. The bystanders took my eyes. There were so many. Except at a horse race or a funeral bystanders in the bush are scarce.

The noise and bustle were enchanting. A labyrinth of streets obscured my sense of direction. Such a lively change from the bush where there was an ache of quietude and every range and road was dulled by familiarity and where one could steer by the sun or stars when outside the usual run.

At Circular Quay, Mrs. Crasterton puffed and I sprang out of the cab where Gaddy, who had arrived on a tram, was awaiting us. Cabs are contraptions designed to defeat all but the sturdiest horses, and the Sydney cab-men were not half so respectable-looking as those of Goulburn, but the ferry boat to North Sydney was a scrumptious dream.

My, the comforts and joys of the city compared with the bush! At Miller's Point, Gaddy dumped us in another cab, which he directed to Geebung Villa, Pannikin Point, and we went off full rip in the wind and rain without him. I craned my neck to see the magnificent rocks rising on one side of the street, covered with the loveliest ferns with little springs of water trickling amongst them. The bamboos waving over walls high above filled me with astonished delight—giants' wands with fairies' grace. Doves were mourning and sparrows were twittering everywhere. On the other side were Aladdin glimpses of the Harbor. All too soon we had arrived.

My hostess paid the cabman. He was not satisfied. "You ugly old buzzard, and two of you and luggage to boot; Had I knowed you were to be that mean, I'd have tipped yous both out in the mud."

"Run inside, my dear," said Mrs. Crasterton.

"You old skin flint, you'd bile down fleas for their hides."

"Run away, you'll be shocked," repeated Mrs. Crasterton, but it seemed cowardly to leave her. The language did not worry me. I had been audience to bullockies in action, to amateurs getting sheep across a creek, and to veterans training sheep puppies. Besides, I have never cultivated the pose that to hear of the common actualities of life would outrage me out of health. It is the being compelled to subscribe to cant and inconsistencies about them that I find so enervating.

A maid took my portmanteau. Mrs. Crasterton told

116

me to follow the maid while she followed me laying the blame of "the growing insolence of the lower classes" on the unhealthy growth of the Labor Party, which she averred would be the ruin of the new Commonwealth. The rain pattered greyly on the bamboos and hibiscus, which shaded the side verandah, the cabby's voice came as a refrain as we entered the home of a dead statesman where I was to find culture and high congeniality.

Only once in a lifetime can anticipation hold such a quality of flattery towards a clique or a class as mine did at that moment.

"We are not having anyone in tonight," said Mrs. Crasterton when she came to my room. "Show me your dresses, child."

It was a trying moment. I showed the new dress that I was to wear in the evenings, and the other one for street wear. "I must give you some dresses," she murmured.

Shame invaded me. "I would rather not," I said shakily. "I could just stay with you. I don't want to see smart people, and then it would not matter about my clothes." My frugal wardrobe merely covered me and the demands of decency, and was in no sense decorative.

I was alone when there was a tap on the door, and there stood a beautiful young lady. "I am Edmée Actem," said she, with a most gorgeous smile. "I'm a bush girl too, and staying here on purpose to meet you. I was born on a station up the country. I just love your book. It's ripping. You've said all the things we all think, but did not know how to express."

Edmée had big bluish grey eyes that she rolled most arrestingly, and her hair was in chestnut curls on her forehead. Her dress showed off her figure in a SOCIETY manner. She was tall "yet voluptuous", just like the

117

heroines in *The Goulburn Evening Penny Post,* and she could languish and cast appealing glances. She looked as if she had all kinds of lovers—quondam, hopeless, distracted and those who would even try to be *clandestine,* and propose to her in *conservatories,* or find her monogrammed handkerchief in the *shrubberies.* Life must begin for me too on meeting her, so lovely and romantic— the very girl of my dreams.

She said she was dressing after dinner. "But that is such a pretty dress, and oh, you are lovely!" burst from me.

She called it just an old rag that she kept for wet nights and when there was no company. Every man who met her must fall madly in love with her. She confirmed this as soon as I confessed apologetically that I had no evening dress. She said it did not matter in my case as I was only a little girl from the bush, but that she was so conspicuous for her fatal beauty that it was an effort to keep pace with it. She knew I would not misunderstand her, and it was a relief to speak from soul to soul without humbug.

I wished that I was so beautiful that men would love me to distraction, but she said I was not the type. I doted and gloated on her while she told me there and then in confidence some of the burdens of her fascination. Such luscious love affairs put my little experiences out of existence.

Right in Geebung Villa Edmée was having trouble. Derek was very troublesome, and would have been the boy of her dreams only that he was four years younger. Gaddy too was a silly old thing. I asked was that why he was called Gaddy, and she laughed and said he had been christened Gad. Derek was a spoiled darling only son, and Gaddy . . . Both lived at Geebung Villa.

I could hardly keep from laughing at the thought of Gad approaching such a beauty as Edmée. In a democracy where admirers abounded by the dozen a girl does not at first realise that a bachelor of any age can purchase a woman of any youth if he but have the wherewithal and determination. It takes time also for a girl to grasp that any old tramp of a man thinks that every woman is craving a man, even a thing like himself, which she wouldn't wipe her boots upon; when all the time her despair is not that she is without men importuning her, but that among the flock there is not one that she could consider with satisfaction, and that the one that she would desire might think her as undesirable as she found the ones who were plaguing her.

Edmée said she was hungry and dissatisfied in her soul, just as I was, and seeking for something other than a mere man. She craved an affinity. We were interrupted by the gong, and Edmée promised to tell me more anon.

The house seemed as big as the Royal Hotel as Edmée took me down with her. Gaddy was waiting to open the dining-room door for us, and wearing a dinner jacket. Mrs. Crasterton was in evening dress, but well-covered in a big shawl and wrestling with a joint. I sat beside Gaddy. Edmée sat opposite. I was glad of that, as I could feast my eyes on her and I hoped that Gad would not mind my being in long sleeves and such a tiny V that it hardly showed any of my neck. Derek did not appear until after we had gone to the library for coffee.

Edmée retired to dress with Wheeler—Mrs. Crasterton's personal maid—in attendance. Derek was being babied in the dining-room and elsewhere, I learned from Gaddy, who had charge of me in the library. Edmée and Derek were going to a ball at Lady Somebody's. This lady herself was chaperoning Edmée as Mrs. Crasterton had a slight chill.

I longed to be helping Edmée to dress, tending her like an altar boy. The incense would have come from my admiration. Derek was all over the place calling to his mother and Gaddy, but I did not catch sight of him. In time he appeared "with 'em all on", as Gaddy said. I did not let my eyes pop too much on beholding him. Here was the beau—the counterpart—of all the heroines embodied in Edmée. He carried a shining topper and snowy gloves, and was in a cloak sort of coat with wings—too swell for words.

He bowed to me from a distance, but charmingly, and smiled with the loveliest teeth. I felt myself beneath his interest and took care not to obtrude. His mother came in and sat near the fire.

"Is she never going to be ready?" he said impatiently, and after a while threw aside his cloak and I saw the perfection of his slimness in the becoming swallow tails. He cursed his tailor, though I thought he must be a virtuoso.

There was no sign of Edmée. Derek went to the piano in the drawing-room and, after half an hour, sent his mother to find out what was keeping "that pestiferous creature". He went into the hall as his mother returned, and complained about being saddled with such a confisticated bore as the ball in the first place, and Edmée as a Woman Friday in the second.

"Dekky darling, you mustn't talk so," said his mother. "Edmée has great influence with Sir George, and you must keep up these connections."

"She always foists herself upon me," grumbled Derek. "Gaddy ought to take his turn. I'd just as soon have

120

stayed at home and played cat's cradle with the infant prodigy."

Derek sounded as if he were dissimulating his passion for Edmée. In another ten minutes she "swept into the room". Her hair was a *coiffure* in which was a pink rose. She was enveloped in a cloak of gold tissue and chiffon and lace. Derek remarked icily that the cab had been waiting an hour, but Edmée wasn't worried or hurried by that. She made lovely flirtatious eyes at Gaddy, kissed me and Mrs. Crasterton and departed.

Mrs. Crasterton disappeared to telephone. Gad played on the piano and showed me books and things, but my heart had gone out for the night with Edmée and Derek. If Derek would give me a few dancing lessons I was sure I could learn in an hour, but it was not natural for such an attractive young man to repair the social deficiencies of a little bush-whacker. The ridicule in his remark about the infant prodigy showed me my place. I longed for just one evening dress. Edmée's wet-night gown would have satisfied me, but Pa hadn't a penny to buy me one and I did not wish to be beholden to Mrs. Crasterton. I did not sleep on going to bed. The day had been packed with experiences, the lights and voices of the Harbor were so alluring, and I thought much of a ball room with an orchestra playing gay waltzes and Edmée and Derek the "cynosure of all eyes".

I was up early. It seemed hours before breakfast. Geebung Villa had terraces to the water's edge, and they were rich with daphne and camellia bushes. The sun came up through the Heads and stole its way to the Quay, far over the bay. Each of the tiny waves turned to flame, and as the sun rose higher it left pearly tracks across the water. A month would not be long enough to imbibe

121

such beauty, and I did not mind a bit that I had no dresses.

Gaddy found me and said that breakfast was nearly ready. He blew his nose like a trumpet and turned about and rattled both hands in his trousers' pockets, and looked as if he would displace his eyes, and then blurted out, "See here, my sister is having a lot of people tonight. Don't you let 'em fuss you. Don't you listen to anything they tell you. You are better than the whole lot of 'em—just as you are."

I was pleased about the people. I longed for people who would be interested in things that I was interested in, and people living in such circumstances and surroundings must surely be they. I did not expect them to worry me, and I certainly intended to listen to all they said. Why should Gaddy give such a queer warning?

Derek and Edmée were both absent from breakfast. Mrs. Crasterton went up to Derek's room while Gad telephoned for a cab, and there was a fuss with a cup of coffee in the hall as Derek later bolted for the cab to race to his office. It was entirely different behaviour from that of young men in the bush—seemed a little *infra dig* for masculinity.

I had established such relations with Edmée that I went to her room while she made her *toilette*. I was impatient to hear of the ball. She and Derek had been the *cynosure*, just as I thought. She was going to lunch with some girl friends at Potts Point, and her dress congested me with superlatives. It was filmy stuff such as worn by the heroines in the *Penny Post*, over a bright colour that *shimmered*, and a lace petticoat. She lifted the fluffy skirts around her ankles in open-work stockings, and she had high-heeled shoes. She had a perfect figure as well

122

as a beautiful face. Her waist was small and her bosom full. She had a spreading picture hat of pleated tulle and feathers, and what she called a *brolly* to match. I revelled in her. She said she had a hard bore of a day ahead of her—lunch and two afternoon teas. There was a new man who was mad about her, of whom I panted to hear, but she departed as soon as she was dressed.

Mrs. Crasterton took me in hand for the day. She said I looked so dainty and girlish, and the real bush maid in my little dresses that it would be a pity to spoil the effect with sophisticated clothes; ordinary girls needed clothes. We lunched at Geebung Villa in solemn state. Mrs. Crasterton said that I must guard against any irreverence for things that mattered or I would not succeed socially.

As a beginning she recited her pedigree. She had descended from a Saxon king. We had a fine pedigree too, containing some moated ruins in Chancery, but Pa always said that a pedigree counted only in stock, as human beings had not sufficient knowledge in eugenics to make it count in themselves yet; that there were too many people living on the reputation of a grandfather while their own works would not bear examination. Pa also held that it was not *descent* in human breed but *ascent* that counted.

Until initiated by Mrs. Crasterton, I had not dreamed that aristocraticness was locally of so much importance.

I knew we had many genuine ladies hidden in remote humpies, while females of feraboracious manners and habits were installed in the mansions of Potts Point, where dwells the nucleus of our aristocracy yet to be—or to be done away with.

I did not enjoy my lunch. It takes great cooking to equal Ma's. Mrs. Crasterton directed my admiration to the antique candle-sticks. The age of the cheese had more

123

pungency. Judged by the normal longevity of cheese, it must have been of such antiquity as to have earned resurrection. It had become a living thing.

Everything hung fire until the evening when Mrs. Crasterton was to be "At Home" to her friends. We were to dress early, have dinner early, and await SOCIETY. Edmée informed me that Mrs. Crasterton was truly of a fine family, though of course slightly inferior to the Actems.

Even in the bush each family I knew was sure of being a little superior to the others. Perhaps it is to obviate such an absence of classification that the society zoo in England is so strictly graded in steps, with a stud book, so that those listed cannot take more than their share of importance.

CHAPTER THIRTEEN.

SOCIETY.

I put on my white dress and stole down. Gaddy was already there, and in swallow tails looked like an egg. I found out later that his nickname was "The Egg". Mrs. Crasterton's head and train promised smartly for what was hidden in the big shawl. Edmée was in her little wet-night dress. There was no trace of Derek, but there was present a small insipid young man with big ears. He was unmistakably infatuated with Edmée. There was also a man about six-foot-two in a violent check suit and long faded walrus moustache.

Mrs. Crasterton had apologised for him as a sort of cousin. She said relations were so huffy that she had to overlook his not being in evening dress, that he was leaving immediately after dinner. He talked in a self-important voice to Jemima, as he call her, and did not see me at all beyond a nod when introduced as "a little girl". His theory was that people of his class, that meant SOCIETY'S and Jemima's, should never touch politics except for what was in them. They should feather their nests and get out while the going was good.

When the meal was eaten Big Ears and Big Checks went to the smoking room with Gaddy. Edmée disappeared upstairs. Mrs. Crasterton had still more telephoning to do, and told me to remain in the drawing-room, as Lady Hobnob was going to run in and see me on her way to a ball at Admiralty House. I must not delay her, as it was kind of her to come.

I wrote in my diary with a fountain pen sent to me by a commercial traveller at Broken Hill, until Gad seated himself nearby with an odour of wine and the stuffed look peculiar to men with short necks and long appetites. My soul did not go out to him. Mrs. Crasterton came in for a moment and said that Edmée's admirer was not of an *old* family, and she pointed out a dog-eared ornament and named the howling swell from whom it had descended.

"Stow that old rubbish, Sis," said Gad testily. "The girl is as young as morning and as fresh as dawn. She doesn't want to concern herself with anything but being herself and not getting spoiled. Age is no recommendation of an article if a new thing would be an improvement. If we are here only to degenerate and breed rotters and find out that old things were better, the sooner we throw up the sponge the better."

I discerned an unexpected ally.

Mrs. Crasterton threw off her shawl to meet arrivals. I was abashed to be in close proximity. Her bosom was like two vast white puddings, her waist was sinfully compressed, she rocked on silly little heels, but she was as fashionable as Wheeler, the expert, could make her. Lady Hobnob was as big as Mrs. Crasterton, but more flabby and spreading. She had her head wrapped in tulle with feathers that nodded precariously, but she was kind. I was sure she must be a muddler. (I had had a *méchante* idea that one bared one's arms and chest to extend one's physical beauty and increase feminine attraction, but the startling exposure of four or five old ladies dispelled this notion. Evening dress must be an obligation of aristocraticness.) The very pronounced human form *au naturel* looks

126

so very pronounced that it would be less of a shock to respectable way-backs to begin EVENING DRESS SOCIETY among slender people. However, the lessons in breeding that I had undergone that day starched my own, and without a blink I continued a when-you-don't-know-what-to-do-do-nothing stand.

Other ladies in grand dresses called for an hour on their way to the ball. They were surprised that I was such a child, and that I had nothing to say for myself. Some said what a pity it was that I would so soon be spoiled. Everyone asked for me, and Mrs. Crasterton said, "Here she is!" Many women kissed me: old gentlemen pinched or goggled and said kind or silly things. Then they settled to talk to Jemima and Gaddy about affairs of the day, and the gossip of Sydney. Some of them were judges, and some were barristers, and M.L.A.'s., and there was a Chancellor, but I don't know of what. Mrs. Crasterton beamed and said it was like old times.

Presently Edmée made her entry. Everyone saw it. She stood for a few minutes in the doorway. She was in a pale green satin dress with a gored skirt with a train and a bodice fitting like a glove. It had no sleeves and was cut very low. Her bosom seemed to rise out of creamy foam. She had a cape of the same satin trimmed with ostrich feathers, and it slipped off in the most exciting way. She languished and distributed her glances. There was a rush from the gentlemen to attend her: but she was true to me. She drew me down beside her where I sat raptly drinking her in. How proud I was when she put her arm around me!

Henry Beauchamp wondered how I'd act when I met girls that could rival me. Here was one who blotted me out, and I was enchanted with her. There was no jealousy in me. I forgot even to be envious; forgot that I was in a plain white dress with all my bath-room charms hidden. I was sorry for Big Ears' hopeless passion for Edmée, and motioned him to come and sit on the other side of me on the couch on which we were sitting. In the crush that ensued around us, I slipped away without being missed. Behind a shoulder of the wall in the back of the long drawing-room I found Big Checks all by himself.

"Hullo!" he said. "You sneakin' out of the ruck too?"

"Yes, I was only taking up space around Miss Actem. Isn't she lovely?"

"A rather upstanding filly. Been a bit too long in the stable. She hangs around here tryin' to bag old Gaddy. She'll bag young Derek if he doesn't keep his eyes skinned."

What a poisonous old man! I knew him at once for a broken-down swell. The bush is full of such. Sometimes they are tramps, but other times they are tea-agents. There was a book-agent around 'Possum Gully, the image of this gentleman, checks, moustache and all. When there is a position as Stock Inspector their relatives use INFLUENCE to get it for them.

"I meant to go after dinner, but Jemima said something about a girl who writes, comin' tonight. I'd as soon have a performin' bear about the place as a woman who writes. The bear's performance would be more natural too."

"Then why did you stay?"

"Thought I'd better see what the world is comin' to. Now that women are to have votes, life won't be worth livin' much longer."

"Do you think that women should not have any brains?"

"Brains! A woman with brains is a monstrosity."

I never can understand why men are so terrified of

women having special talents. They have no consistency in argument. They are as sure as the Rock of Gibraltar that they have all the mental superiority and that women are weak-minded, feeble conies; then why do they get in such a mad-bull panic at any attempt on the part of women to express themselves? Men strut and blow about themselves all the time without shame. In the matter of women's brain power they organise conditions comparable to a foot race in which they have all the training and the proper shoes and little running pants, while women are taken out of the plough, so to speak, with harness and winkers still on them, and are lucky if they are allowed to start at scratch. Then men bellow that they have won the race, that women never could, it would be against NATURE if they did. Surely it is not brave to so fear fair play. No self-respecting woman could possibly *respect* men, no matter how strong an appetite she might have for them, but to be sorry for them, as some women pretend, is mawkish, and is carrying dissimulation too far.

Big Checks would put me on a level with a performing bear, and never know the alphabet of my language, but I could talk his pidgin while thinking about something else, so I indulged him on the subject of horses.

It was evident that he was a full bachelor. He lacked the mugginess of husbands and the air of false importance which they assume through the protection of their wives. Why women can be led astray by others' husbands or have any traffic with them I cannot conceive.

"I heard about this girl," I said.

"By jove, do you know her! Tell me what she is like."

He was greedily interested for that sort of bachelor which the women don't try to attract as compared with the sort that they do.

"I believe her book was meant as a joke, but people couldn't see it. Her relations say that she is a silly goat and that her book is just like her."

"I knew it. No nice girl would write a book."

"I wish I could write one—only of course a much better one than this girl has done."

"Oh, no, my dear, don't be led astray by the false adulation and fuss about this minx. People come to look at her like a Punch and Judy show, but the kind of girl the world is in need of, the kind a man respects is one just like your pretty little self."

Nevertheless he had not come to see her but the dreadful female who wrote.

"Me, pretty," I scoffed. "My mother doesn't say so."

"Ah, you have a sensible mother. She wants to save you from conceit. You take it from me, and I've seen all the girls come out for the last twenty-five years, there's not many could hold a candle to you if you were properly tricked out. You have a face that grows on a man—something that would make him come back and look a second time; and no paint or artificiality."

"Think how lovely Miss Actem is," I said to end his embarrassing exaggeration.

"Pooh! Your figure and complexion run her into the Harbor, and her eyes . . . "

"They're glorious."

"Go and look at your own. The way she ogles and throws hers about—I'm afraid, 'pon me word, that they'll drop out and I'll have to pick 'em up."

No doubt he had been snubbed by Edmée for getting in the way of more interesting cavaliers. He babbled of how the world would be dished by female suffrage. Women were never meant to express themselves politically;

they were born to sacrifice themselves—that was their glory and their crown: as soon as women began to assert themselves a nation declined.

I hung on secretly to my faith that the greatest nations would always be those where women were freest. The United States and the British Empire were the two countries where women could march about alone without being assailed by the men, and even BIG CHECKS and LOUDER CHECKS would agree that the English are the greatest race on earth, and themselves the most wonderful men.

Mrs. Crasterton found me as she came through to give some order about the refreshments. "Dear me, Obadiah," she remarked, "was it you that abducted the guest of the evening? Everyone wants to talk to you, Sybylla. You must not hide yourself."

BIG CHECKS stood up and said, "I can't wait any longer for this performin' bear". He grunted as if he had said something smart and funny. "I've enjoyed myself so much with you that she would spoil the taste in my mouth. Look here, don't you go worryin' because you haven't any brains, me dear: You're perfect as you are."

"I don't worry for lack of brains," I said demurely.

"That's right, you leave brains to this performin' bear with long teeth, and a thick waist, and about ten feet high." He was again so pleased with his joke that I laughed at him, and he shook my hand very friendlily and went out by the hind door, took his cane and hat and let himself out.

Mrs. Crasterton, Gaddy, Edmée and I were finally left before the dying fire.

"Well, my dear, you are a huge success," Mrs. Crasterton said to me. "I hope your dear little head won't be turned by being the lion of the hour. Everyone has invited me to bring you to lunch or afternoon tea. People whom I had lost sight of since Papa died, came tonight, and smart people who have arisen since my young days have telephoned that they must meet you. Dear old Lady Hobnob is so taken with you that I am to take you to her big dinner tomorrow night and you are to spend the night with her. The literary people and artists are clamoring for you like the hungry lions at the zoo, but I don't approve of the bohemians: they have dangerous political views and are loose in their morals."

It was not disguised from me that my good behaviour had been a surprise. I had not shown the shock of disappointment on finding that people who had enjoyed opportunities of education, travel, "contact" and refinement, which had long been debarred me owing to indigence, were only like this. There weren't any but Derek and Edmée who took my eye, and I heard Gaddy having quite a row with his sister about Edmée.

I sat by my window looking on the city across the Harbor for a long time. It all seemed unreal. A myriad lights shone like misty jewels across the balmy water where the ferry boats flitted like floating fires. It was all so beautiful that I resented more tensely than ever that so much of my life had been cramped into the ugly environs of 'Possum Gully.

Edmée was up betimes next morning. I heard her talking to the others as I approached. "I was in hopes she would be more the *enfant terrible,* but she is too correct to be entertaining."

"Wait till she comes out of her shell," said Gaddy.

"I like her affection, and she is not a troublesome guest," said Mrs. Crasterton. "Professor Jonathan says she promises more genuis than anyone in the Colonies today, and Lady Hill says she would take Professor Jonathan's word before anyone's. He is a really cultured Englishman, and it is a pleasure to hear him say ninety-nine."

"Go on, Sis!" said Gaddy good-humoredly, "He says nainty-nain."

Chapter Fourteen.

Hi-Tiddly-Hi-Ti-Hi!

I was all on tip-toe for the dinner of Lady Hobnob. The Hobnobs were described by one of the English guests of the "at home" night as able "to do things rather well for the Colonies." This meant that they had the money and EXPERIENCE to give dinners of many courses including decayed game and several kinds of wine served by the regulation number of imported flunkeys.

The whole toot was going to this dinner. We went a little early so that my host could have an additional word with me. He became noisy on finding that I was the daughter of good old Dick Melvyn, one-time Member for Gool Gool, "One of the straightest men who ever lived, but ideas ahead of the times, and no head for business." So that was his idea of Pa's ideals. I let him do the shouting, and soon we went in to dinner.

There was a glare of bosoms above the table and much superfluous drapery lying around the chair legs underneath, and hardly one dish out of the long list of courses that was sweet and wholesome enough for my palate so it must have been a *recherché* meal.

I sat on old Sir Jimmy's left, a married woman had to have his right, but he grinned at me and talked to me most of the time. He declared that he never read a novel, but proclaimed that I was a ripping little girl and would soon settle down in marriage and leave scribbling to men or to those women who couldn't catch a man. Such pid-

134

gin exposed his attitude towards women. His small talk was small indeed, even when he enlarged it by discussing probabilities for the Melbourne Cup. So he was easy to humour, and we got on swimmingly until he began about his wines. He was a connoisseur, and prided himself on his cellar.

"Come, come! You must drink wine at my table," said he, with pompous geniality.

"No thank you, Sir James."

"You must, my dear. You must."

"No thank you," I said firmly.

"Have you principles against drinking wine?"

"No, but I don't like it, thank you."

"Then you must learn to like it."

Edmée was signalling for me to drink it, but my fighting blood was up. I had had to sink to his level about writers, which was most insulting to artistic intelligence and the rights of women. I would go no lower to please him, especially as I was feeling very resentful inside, and despising him as a swindler of public funds, who had thereby grown rich and important — with his gluttonous dinners and snifty servants! — while Pa's honesty had resulted in deprivation and failure.

"Now, now, I insist," persisted Sir James.

Poor old Gaddy was red in the face. Derek was pretending not to hear.

I shook my head and looked modest, which further incited Sir James. "Can you give me one good reason why you should not drink my wine?"

"Yes. If you came to see Pa and Ma and me we wouldn't have any wine because we could not afford it. Pa tried to do good for his fellows and lost his money. We could offer you nothing better than tea and coffee and if you did not like them we would be sorry but we would not pester you to drink them against your wish."

Sir James patted me on the hand and said, "Plucky little filly. If you were entered at Randwick you would run away from the field. I'll drink your health out of a damned feeding bottle. What I like in women or horses is mettle."

Later in the drawing-room he sat beside me and said that while Lady Hobnob was away in Melbourne he would give a dinner specially for me with no damned married women present, so that I could have the place of honour. He smelt and looked as though he had drunk my share of the wine in addition to his own. Ill-bred old toad!

Why should one be plagued to drink alcohol but allowed to refuse coffee or tea without any buzz?

I did not look forward to Sir Jimmy's company when the guests left but he was in bed snoring ten minutes after the last goodnight. Lady Hobnob said they were old campaigners and had such a heavy social round that they did their best to curtail late hours.

Breakfast was brought to my bed by a maid, but I dressed before eating. It seemed frowsy to eat in bed as if I were ill. The maid later took me to her ladyship's room where she was sitting up with the remains of a meal and many letters and papers scattered on her bed. This was an off day, by a miracle, and she was giving it to me because she had been moved by my book. She said that once she too had been a little girl in the bush who had thought that the great world would be wonderful.

"And now," I glowed, "You have met all the great people and have seen Queen Victoria as well as King Edward and Queen Alexandra."

She had been home to both Jubilees as a Government

guest and to the Coronation, and told me of the wonders of Buckingham Palace and Windsor Castle, but wound up "It has been a long weary way, my dear, from the old bush track with the mopokes calling and the moon coming up over the back paddock, and you brought me home to my youth."

I stayed to lunch with her alone. I liked her, though she suggested untidiness. She was a bit gone about the belt and straggly around the hem, and not above grubbiness in the lace at wrists and neck, and her hat was dowdy.

You should see Ma's belts, and her hems and her lace! She is always the pink of perfection (her own phrase) even when she is baking, or washing the blankets. From Ma I had gathered the idea that to be unkempt about hem or belt was the equivalent of being weak-minded, and Ma was emphatic that daintiness of person, especially when women were elderly, was indispensable.

I hate to have to mention anything so low, but it had a big influence on my attitude, so it must go in. I found that Hobnob House had BUGS. Yes, insects that are never mentioned except in soft pedal and with a nick-name B FLATS. The vegetables at lunch tasted of antique butter and there was a mouldy atmosphere in the top floors. No one as capable as Ma had been there. It appeared that Lady Hobnob specialised in big dinners for which caterers and waiters came in. There were lots of other things that would have made Ma and Grandma snort in Hobnob Villa and the other houses I saw later.

When we were at dinner at Geebung Villa after my return, Edmée took me to task for provincialism in refusing Sir James's wine, and Mrs. Crasterton said I must guard against being tiresome and odd or showing any

137

taint of socialism. Only Gaddy cheered me still.

"You had a case," said he. "You have a right to your own tastes and old Jimmy was rude. As for the crowd they'd dress in sugee bagging if some bigger swell took the lead."

I sat silent and rather stubborn. I would have adduced the B FLATS only that Lady Hobnob had been so kind. I thought about them, however, and resisted SOCIETY pretensions. Pa and Ma had reared me exceptionally, plus which I had my own affliction of bringing reality to bear. After all, my paternal grandmother had been assured of her altitude above the hoi polloi of the "beastly Cawlonies"; and a cockatoo's crest would have been an infant compared with the eyebrows of my maternal grandfather had Sydney society tried to dictate his right to tolerate it or to ignore it.

As I retreated upstairs I heard Gaddy again, "If she weren't different from other girls she wouldn't be such a draw, and you would have to give her some new dresses. I never met another kid who would have the pluck to go among others all dressed to kill while she has nothing but the one school-girl dress of some kind of white rag."

I was continually surprised by Gaddy's understanding: but ah, if Derek had only championed me! Gaddy put on no airs about literature and we both loved flowers, so we had an absorbing topic in common. He was responsible for the beauty of the terraced gardens and dug in them himself on Saturdays and Sunday mornings. He was something in a Government Department — a soft job, I was told, with a big screw that his brother-in-law had secured for him while in power.

Sunday. Mrs Crasterton asked Edmée and me to accompany her to church. Edmée laboured in a Sunday

138

school while in Sydney. "Horrible little brutes of kids!" she observed. "I detest them, but it is good to keep in with the Church. Sometimes the most distinguished people from England have introductions that keep them tight in church circles. Besides, men say that a girl without religion is like a rose without perfume."

This sort of yelp raised in me a devil of opposition and I decided to tell any man that began to admire me that I was a free-thinker.

My hostess appeared in a black satin gown and a resplendent yellow bonnet and a set of "wonderfully old" jewellery, and carried a prayer book inscribed by the Bishop. I chose to stay at home with Gaddy. I did not feel well-dressed enough for church.

Gaddy read a yellow-back in French and I read the *Sunday Times*. In it I found a story about myself. Some writer under an *alias* said I had no idea of how to dress. She ridiculed my appearance among fashionable people in a dress suitable only for the house in the morning, and flat-heeled shoes and cotton stockings, and said that I had no cloak but a sort of jacket, and that my hands showed the effects of manual labour, and that I had no idea of how to exercise sexual charm. She also said that nothing could have excited more interest than my lack of a suitable wardrobe.

"What does exercising sexual charm mean?" I asked Gaddy.

He damned and exploded and said he had meant to burn that unholy rag, and that exercising charm meant rolling one's eye like Edmée did, and exposing the salt-cellars around the clavicles, and having a lot of damned rags on the floor where he was forever tripping over 'em.

This SOCIETY REPORTER was a Mrs. Thrumnoddy

who had been at the Hobnobs' dinner, and considered herself the best-dressed woman in Sydney. "Does she get money for writing like that about me?" I asked.

Gaddy said she certainly did, and was the wife of a rich broker.

No wonder she could dress well!

"Gaddy," I said, "I could dress well if I had money, but the drought killed all our stock, and Pa is not a good business man. We haven't a thing really. I couldn't even have a sash for my dress, but my stockings are real good cashmere." I began to cry.

"Never mind, ducky," said he. "Your little finger is worth all those old cats put together. Do let us get you some clothes. My sister owes it to you for all the social prominence you are bringing her."

I shrank into my shell. A man offering me clothes filled me with shame, even though it was only fat old Gaddy, who seemed more like Humpty Dumpty than a man or a bachelor or even an uncle. I longed for pretty clothes but could bear up without them, what cut me so deeply was that a woman who had kissed me and made such a fuss over me could write about me like that in the paper for everyone to read, and that she could get money for writing thus while I could not get any for writing about her, though I needed it so dreadfully. I hate unfairness.

Gaddy said no more. He got books and read to me. His reading was feraboracious, but his kindness soothed like oil on a burn. As we were going in to lunch, he said that I was not to mind Mrs. Thrumnoddy, that she was a petty parasite who had had the opportunity of her life in meeting me.

Even the Harbor with the white sails on it and the ferries all gay with clothes and busking men could not rescue Sunday from being a stale day. Young Mr. Big Ears came home from church with Edmée and Mrs. Crasterton. Gaddy said that he was a teacher in the Sunday School and that was why Edmée laboured in that vineyard.

Big Ears brought two boxes of chocolates, an enormous one, which he handed to me, and a tiny one which he handed to Edmée. When we were alone I said he had made a mistake, but Edmée said no, she had asked him to give me this as she hated chocolates, but Big Ears evidently thought it would look queer to leave her out altogether.

On Monday, Mrs Crasterton took me sightseeing. We looked at the shops and she gave me a little imitation gold brooch which delighted me, as I had no other. I dragged her everywhere from the Post Office Tower to a waxworks show. She was a kind victim, as she was old and heavy. I loved it all, though I was haunted by a sense of delinquency in doing anything but the wash on Monday. Monday with me had always been sacred to the laundry and Sunday's scraps, except when Christmas despotically fell on a Monday.

It was such a busy day that I had no time to brood on the writing woman's pricks, and when we got home there was a parcel awaiting me — the most wonderful necklace and bracelets, heavy and old-fashioned and valuable. They were from Big Ears. He said they had been his mother's so that he could not give them to me outright yet, but that he had heard me say that I loved bracelets and it would be a great honour to him if I wore these while in Sydney.

This looked like another kindness *grace à Edmée*. Big Ears had also left a note for Mrs. Crasterton. As it was an off night he hoped she would be free and that he might take her and me to a concert to hear a budding Melba. Edmée said, "By jove, I'm glad you are rescuing me from that screech owl, and I do hope Big Ears will soon come to a head so that I can get rid of him."

Derek had a similar idea of Big Ears. When his mother said that Big Ears was interested in me because he too was a writer, Derek snorted uproariously. He was having dinner with us for the first night since my arrival.

"Dekky, don't be naughty. He wrote charming verses in my album. He is one of our minor poets."

Already we had met no end of poets — the big fellows one at a time, that is if Mrs. Crasterton thought them "nice" enough to be exposed to my unsophistication. We had the damned little twinkling stars in constellations at tea to produce a stellary effect.

"Big Ears doesn't look like a poet," I exclaimed. Messrs Lawson, Paterson, Brady, Quinn, Ogilvie and others set a high standard of physique which outclassed poor little Big Ears.

"Look like a poet! He looks like a greengrocer's assistant who — who teaches Sunday School," ended Derek.

Gaddy had a stunning blue sash waiting for me. I longed to own it but had not been educated to receive things. Mine was the independence which loves to lavish gifts upon others but squirms at receiving them. The sash was so long and my middle inches so few that I had to put the sash twice around me, and then it covered me to the armpits, and the ends of the big bow fell to the hem of my skirt. The cook, who was a darling, had done up my little dress and it was all fresh and glistening. Gaddy said that the sash was no more than a box of chocolates, and with a laugh added, that I could at least borrow

142

it while I was in Sydney if I wouldn't take it altogether. I consented to wear it until I could write and ask Ma if I could keep it.

CHAPTER FIFTEEN.

MY TRUE FRIEND.

Being too young and too poor to make a formal début,
I was an anomaly. Other youngsters as poor as I already
had their shoulders to the working wheel; those of financial
status were acquiring extra polish to enhance their value
in the matrimonial market. I had not 'come out', but was
a chicken that walked around inside its shell — a
good simile, seeing my lack of an evening dress. I was
treated like a visitor of thirty or fifty years of age. Without
any fuss or feathers I was just tucked in at dinners and
luncheons, and people called to see me by the score. Quite
two-thirds were men and half of them over forty. It was
rare that there was a youngster of my own youth amid
the throng. A great many talked about nothing; others
exclaimed, "Oh, how interesting!" People were not described as pretty or clever or entertaining or queer but as
interesting. I grew very sick of this description of myself,
but had quickly perceived that it was wiser to think what
I said than to say what I thought.

I met numerous men, each of whom had written "that
beautiful thing" or "this beautiful thing," each thing according to some authority, being the best thing that had
been done since Pope or Dryden or Keats, and the authors
designated as the Australian Poe, or Burns or Milton. I
was in an uncomfortable predicament owing to my ignorance of all this Australian genius, but I had no difficulty
in getting the geniuses on to the subject of their own
supremacy and thus hiding my own inferiority.

144

People asked silly questions about myself. I had brought this to pass by pronunciamentos upon the desirability of honesty in egotism. In this way I found a new angle in the workings of egotism. I did not mind what I said about myself as a subject impersonally, while I stood aloof like a scientist in his laboratory, but I resisted when outsiders tried to intrude behind my reserve. I developed much ingenuity in turning the tables.

One man peristed, "Why, when you speak so frankly against humbug in egotism, why do I find you the most difficult, the most shrinking, little creature I ever met? Can you explain?"

I couldn't. I can't.

Perhaps there are two divisions of egotism, one the absorption in self as self, the other the analysis of self as part of a universal complex force, and I am an analyst rather than the normal egotist.

As one of those old professor birds, with less gift for obscurity than usual among the academic, has said, "Criticism means self-consciousness, and self-consciousness means renewed activity on a higher plane. The reflective play of one age becomes the passion of another."

There was an article about me in a paper that I had not previously known of, but it had a big circulation in Sydney by currying scandals about people of prominence. The Editor said that Sydney people showed their general degeneracy in running after each new thing as it was advertised. Sybylla Melvyn's dreadful book had been written in six weeks, and when he expressed his disapproval people said, "Yes, but it was wonderful for a girl of sixteen." Then he felt as Dr. Johnson towards the *difficult* musical performance which he wished had been *impossible*. The

Editor asserted that I had begun as a conceited and self-assertive hoyden and the foolish lionising of Sydney SOCIETY had confirmed and developed me into an obnoxious specimen.

This was interesting and did not hurt like Mrs. Thrumnoddy's defection towards a fellow guest. I went to Gaddy. He spluttered. "Did that man ever see me?" I inquired Gaddy said no, that he was the real scum, that his jealousy in not being able to get within coo-ee of me had inspired this attack. I said if he had ever met or even seen me he would be entitled to his opinion however harsh or undiscerning, but as he hadn't, there was the rub, because before I had got into print, I had, like other innocents, depended upon the printed word, and another bulwark was going bung. The accusation that I advertised myself was particularly unwarranted. I had no acquaintance among newspaper people, and did not give so much as a backward glance to make myself conspicuous. My strenuous endeavour was to be as inconspicuous as possible.

"Is that Sydney SOCIETY I have been meeting?" I asked.

Gad said I could bet my sweet life it was; not only the nice old parliamentary people and the University professors but some of the real smart-setters among whom even riches would not always buy an entry. There was disillusionment in finding that I had to reef in my standards to be at home here. It was now that I felt the force of Pa's tenet that Ma was a wonderful woman. I did not come in contact with anyone of Ma's ability and appearance.

I had hours to put in while Wheeler dressed Mrs. Crasterton, and I wrote in my diary or pondered discontentedly on the waste it was that Ma could not have a nice town house. It was a heinous thing for all Ma's administrative

146

ability to be squeezed into a petty grind of one irreverent urchin, one rebellious girl and one gentle and easily-pleased man. Ma could have managed a grand hotel or some vast institution, and in the place unto which it had pleased God to mis-direct her she had but a poverty-restricted cubby. No doubt she had found the same luny obstructions to using her ability as I had run my head into with mine.

I was desperately in need of money. If I had had the means I should have been a recluse, but when you are poor you are helpless to build a barrier to keep people away. I stood it as quietly as I could. I told Mrs. Crasterton that I had imposed upon her hospitality long enough, I would now like to go home.

She positively wailed that that would make a fool of her. All of Sydney that had not met me was clamoring to do so, including the Admiral; and some of these high official invitations were really commands. I was tired of high officials and longed for young people like Derek and Edmée. I sometimes played the piano while they practised new steps in the hall. If I could play tennis and dance, and have just one evening dress to show my *décolleté* I was sure I could have some fun coloured by a little of the romance that swirled around Edmée. When I went swimming the girls always said that the more clothes I took off the prettier I grew. I wished that Derek would give me a lesson in dancing, but his hopeless passion for Edmée's fatal beauty so burdened him that he thought of me only to play the piano so that he could "hold her in his arms."

Mrs. Greville de Vesey put the cap on my society rights regardless of the frock of "some kind of white rag", and my cotton (cashmere) stockings. Her mother had been born on the station adjoining my mother's, and knew that

147

Ma was as high as herself. Mrs. de Vesey was the chic leader of the younger smart set. People were no longer surprised that I was so properly behaved, my mother being one of the lovely Misses Bossier of Caddagat, which is one of the few original stations entered in the *Landholders' Record*. The Melvyns too were among the earliest educated free men to take up stations in the Southern District. It was I who was entitled to look into other people's pretensions to being of the old squattocracy.

Mrs. de Vesey said that banana-barrow and bottle-o commercialism did not yet rule SOCIETY in Sydney though it was going that way. I loved Zoë de Vesey. She reminded me of a cruiser cutting a clean high wave and sending barges and lesser craft scuttling to their lesser ways. With the Governor-General to announce that I was a genius, and Zoë to vouch for my antecedents, I was established. Zoë said that I need not be shy about imposing on Mrs. Crasterton. Poor old soul had sunk into "innocuous desuetude" following the death of her husband, and this was a happy revival for her. She was really of good family, and Gaddy was a bachelor whom all the girls tried to bag.

"Bag Gaddy!!"

"Gaddy is rich. Edmée Actem camps there every now and again, but he hasn't given in yet. He'd be a fine instrument for an ambitious woman."

"He's silly about Edmée," I said. "But she cannot be bothered with him."

Zoë laughed her short mocking laugh, "You are taking Edmée at her own valuation."

Zoë was almost young, not more than twenty-eight and I loved going to her house and talking to her.

My wearing the jewellery of Big Ears brought me fresh attention. He too was rich, though not of high aristocraticness. His father had made his money in mines. Big Ears had been sent to Cambridge to acquire gentility and was to go into Parliament to establish himself. People seemed to gather importance under Zoë's classification, though I had discerned nothing much in them when trying to place them by my own INEXPERIENCE. Her estimate of people was out of EXPERIENCE mixed with CONTACT. She summed them up by what they *did* and *had*. I could only measure them by what they *were*. When I saw Mrs. Crasterton booming across a drawing-room I measured that she was of exactly the same proportions and human texture as Mrs. McSwat, save that Mrs. Crasterton had had some sort of a tilling and wore expensive stays, whereas Mrs. McSwat's form was unconfined and her culture had camped out at Barney's Gap and subsisted on bully and damper. I saw that the brass buttons and uniforms of the Admiral's staff, which have a dangerous charm for the fair, were worn by boys of helplessly English posture and stilted speech. Some of them were clean cut and straight of limb, but I could see that there were any number of bullock drivers, shearers and boundary riders of my acquaintance in patched shirts and thrummy moles who matched them muscle for muscle and thew for thew.

Soon the people who had predicted that I would be ruined by adulation were croaking that there was something the matter with me as I was not impressed by anyone or anything, that I was very difficult, and laughed at the most important people and made friends of those of no substance, just because I liked them. I would never advance by such tactics.

At the end of my first ten days in SOCIETY my true friend hove above the horizon of my bantling career. Ma had warned me that those who flattered me would not

149

be my true friends, they would want only to get something out of me. My true friends would correct me for my good. Mr. Wilting so mangled the vanity I did not have, that there was no mistaking his good intentions.

He was a pugnacious old boy who did a lot of reviewing on the *Watchdog,* a paper not so long born, with the reputation of possessing the only literary acumen in the new Commonwealth. The sole reason that Mr. Wilting was to be found in the crude wilds of the Antipodes was to better his health. This, I inferred, though exile for him was likely to be the making of Australian literature.

He orated from the hearthrug, standing. "My dear child, I have read your book and discern in it germs of genius. If fostered and cultivated these may bear fruit in time."

This was opposed to the point of view that marriage would take literary prankishness out of me.

"Of course you are very crude. Your workmanship does not exist. You must start from the a b c. I wish I could have the forming of your style. I don't know of anyone else in these beastly Cawlonies who wouldn't ruin you."

"Do you think women *ever* could write?" I inquired in a very small voice.

"Madam," said he, drawing his chest upwards and twirling his mustache, "the immortal Sappho was a woman."

"Yes, but Shakespeare is claimed as a man. Men always say there is no female Shakespeare."

"Humph! You study the fellows who say that, and you'll see they are a long way from being Shakespeares themselves. Why shouldn't women have the same privilege?"

Good for the old boy! After that I did not care how he strutted. He had won my affection.

"You'll never do work that will live if you listen to your friends — *so-called* friends. They will gush over you and call you a genius. Don't listen to them; and as for the literary talent of Australia, there is none. Unfortunately the literary men of Sydney are neither *literary* nor *men.* Even your University professors are only third-rate fellows —men who could never rise out of the ruck if they remained in England, so they came out here where they can lord it in a tin-pot circle."

Mr. Wilting had stated that his health was the reason of his own exile.

"The wife of one of our Governors said there is no society in Australia," I murmured.

"She was right. Neither is there any culture. Neither are there any *literati.* There is only a set of local cacklers unknown out of their own barn. You will quickly set in the same crude limitations unless you can gain a perspective. You must burst the bonds of your environment. In your childish ignorance you are over-awed by the tinkling horse-rhymes and bullock-driving jingles of these fellows. They are beneath consideration from a literary point of view. The crudeness of the average Australian is appalling — appalling! and his cocksureness prevents his improvement."

In many a friendly bush home the more tender of the poems decried by this gentleman were copied by girls into their albums and were treasured as the only expression of familiar emotions and scenes, while the more rousing couplets were often on the lips of their brothers and gave a little colour to arid monotony as they ploughed, ringbarked, shore, milked and put up the heavy fences. Around the camp fires far out this gentleman could have heard the work of these poets he despised enlivening the bare

151

nights of the unfurnished pioneer life. I plucked up courage to voice my conviction that in another generation or two these Australian ballads would be lauded as being as typically Colonial as Burns's were Scottish. I held that our poets were our folklore-ists, and worthy of all the affection we gave them. I ventured to suggest that perhaps the English mind, to its loss, did not extract the essence of Australianism.

Oh, my! what I brought upon myself! Mr. Wilting said that what he feared was true. I had the Australian cocksureness, was so crudely self-opinionated that I could never improve. The only thing to save me would be immediate transplantation to England, where I would find my level before my mind became set.

"But," I persisted, becoming possessed of a devil, as Ma used to say, "why should everything English be our model just because it is English? Shouldn't we do something on our own hook?"

"*On our own hook!*" he repeated with a shudder. "To quote some of your own doggerel-mongers,

> * *'But objects near the vision fill,*
> *When one forgets the things afar;*
> *A jam tin on the nearest hill*
> *When touched by sunlight seems a star."*

"But that seems to be on your side," I suggested.

"He has gropings. He's not quite so cocksure."

I had met Mr. Wilting's mentality before. Plenty of it had penetrated to 'Possum Gully. Such people's families found Australia a handy dumping-ground for their misfits and undesirables, but the silly dumpedees instead of having the spunk to help us natives do something *on our own hook*

* *"Bulletin" Verse.*

152

in Australianism, thought we should all imitate the English most lickspittlingly. Of course we are proud of our English heritage, than which, sad to say, there is no better. By that I mean that it is depressing that it is the best that man has achieved at present, but hang it all, one *is* a bit of a crawler not to be *something on one's own hook*. It's a jolly good phrase, and we must achieve something better than servile imitation to be worthy of England and Shakespeare.

Mr. Wilting shook his head at me. Well he might, had he known what I really contained in the way of ideas: but with one part of myself I thought it most kind of him to stoop to me at all. At least he did not want to extirpate my idea of writing, he merely wanted to direct it and change its personality. I was grateful for this, but thought him rather a confisticated bore and an obsolete frump in his other strains. I ventured to ask if I could earn a few shillings like other people by writing articles. He said to be sure I could, I should write an article about my own views and send it to him. This filled me with hope.

Having eaten all the cakes and sandwiches which Mrs. Crasterton had left me to dispense so that this culture-engendering CONTACT might be undiluted, he took up his hat and stick and said, "You know nothing about love. Keep off the subject until you mature; though study will help you a little, and you'll need practice. I hope to see a great improvement in your love-making next book: it is very crude in this one, very crude indeed."

"It's exactly the way men make love," I maintained.

"That's the reason it's a failure as art — mere raw material — crude." With this puzzling statement he clapped his hat crudely on his head shook my hand and departed.

If I put down what really happened when men were spoony, why should that be crude? Well, at any rate I had had lots of practice in love — in being loved — since I had perpetrated that fake autobiography.

To escape Mrs. Crasterton's sententiousness as to how much I should have learned from a man like that, and to begin on the article, I betook myself to my own room. Gaddy was sitting in his study with the door open as I passed, having just come home by cab. He often called me in to ask what measure I had taken of things. I threw away caution with him as I felt I could trust him. His fatness made him safe and kind, and he was always on my side.

"What kind of an old frogabollow is that?" I demanded.

"He's one of the geni-asses from HOME. They send us a good supply. They fill the vacancies left by our crude youngsters who go to put punch into the effete old world."

Gad emphasised the word crude with a wink. "The pressure of competition or tippling drives them out to us. We haven't the population to make an arena for our men of art or letters or other kinds of ability, so they go to the central market. This old chap is right in some things, but in others he's a decadent blitherer, and when our young fools try to reflect his point of view it quite breaks 'em up."

I felt like hugging Gaddy, but refrained because he did not enjoy interruption in the middle of a discourse.

"I think, meself, there's something in imagining the greatness of an undeveloped country, but old Wilting measures greatness by the style of clubs and art galleries, and dismisses the menace of the slums as being inevitable for the lower orders."

"He says Australia has no background."

"And England has so much that she is a museum of

154

what has been, while Australia is an experimental laboratory of what will be. I prefer foreground to background."

"He says the lovemaking in my book is crude. Miss Elderberry and Mrs. Swift said that too."

"It's a fact, me dear. There is the same difference between your idea of love-making and the experience of those old warhorses as there is between an English breakfast and a French dinner. To gain the approval of those destriers you would need to have love made to you by none except those who should not approach you — other women's husbands for instance."

"That would be disgusting. I wouldn't listen."

Gaddy laughed till he cried, but I could not see why. "You should be able to incite *amour* and extract the erotic excitement from it without running amok of the conventions or the tongues of those experienced in detecting smart love. You'll find plenty of fellows so skilled in lovemaking that they can put a double end on it, so that if you know how to give experienced encouragement they are prepared to go the whole length; but if you are found to be of honest virtue they can take the down off the situation and leave you to feel that you had been the one in the wrong. Thank God you are crude, as crude as your lily and roses complexion that can bear the sun's crude morning glare, and crude may you remain as long as possible, is my prayer."

CHAPTER SIXTEEN.

A GREAT NAME IN AUSTRALIAN LITERATURE.

From that date I began to have more practice in love, or perhaps it was merely experience.

The following morning I posted my article to Mr. Wilting, then opened my mail. In it was a long letter from Big Ears. He told me that he loved me to distraction. Every day since I had come to town he had perched in a Moreton Bay fig in his grounds which overlooked our route to the ferry, to watch me go by. Would I, could I ever think of him? He would have patience for ten years if necessary. I was shocked. What would Edmée think — when she had been so kind to me! Fortunately she despised him, and was waiting for him to propose solely to dismiss him. With another section of myself I thought, Huh! if I put this down, Mr. Wilting would say I know nothing of how men make love.

I hadn't time to think just then: the telephone rang and Mrs. Crasterton called me. "You had better hear the whole of this," she said. "I find you are a wise young thing and seem to know more than those who are trying to instruct you."

She handed me the second ear piece. Zoë de Vesey was speaking.

Now it appears that Australia has one great literary man, or that one great literary man was a native of Australia? He had been many years in London, had gone HOME on the Press Association but in London had had

156

the opportunity to turn into a real man of letters. He was now one of the most successful playwrights of the day. His plays had record runs in London. Here was a comet with two tails when compared with the LOCAL CACKLERS. He made pots of money, Zoë said, but his expensive tastes kept ahead of his income. He went everywhere and was a social lion. And this great god had expressed the wish to see little me during his visit to his native land.

He had been born on the Northern Tableland as I on the Southern, but he had gone to the University and had swum about in SOCIETY since a tadpole, whereas I had simply been entitled to do so, but had been kept on the cockatoo level because of indigence.

At the time of the Diamond Jubilee he had won a prize for an ode entitled, *Australia to England!,* and became known as the Australian Swinburne. However, he had quickly renounced all Australian crudities and had written a novel of London entitled *The Woman Who Wilted,* one of the greatest circulating library successes, which had earned him the title of the Australian Anthony Hope.

"He doesn't seem to be anything *on his own hook*", thinks I to myself.

On going to London he had not stressed his Australian origin but played the game on London lines. He had outdone the Londoners in Londonness through having more of England known in knowing Australia too. His comedies of duchesses and high ladies who knew all about extracting the erotic excitement from *amour,* as Gaddy put it, were the last word in being risque without being bannable. He was a SUCCESS. He must be just reeking with EXPERIENCE, thinks I, drinking in this titillating news.

He had had to fight for long years in London for recog-

157

nition, and might never have won it only that he had got away as a war correspondent for the *Daily Thunderer* for a year with the Boers, and his articles had charmed everyone. He was a sizzling imperialist. Rhodes had condescended to him, Kipling patted him on the back, Barney Barnato nudged him in the ribs. He was on the way to a title and all that. What he needed to complete him was a wealthy and influential marriage. Only now could he afford to emphasise his Australian nativity and turn it to commercial account.

He had always kept in touch with the Press Association and while out was to do some articles on Australia from an imperial angle which would appear in *The Thunderer* and *The Argus,* or perhaps it was *The Age,*—I can't tell these two apart. He was also connected with a leading publishing house, and if he saw anything worth picking up, was to pick it up. This gave him great importance among us poor LOCAL CACKLERS, of which I was the localest and least. If he could, without compromising his status and deteriorating his attainments, he would insert an Australian character or scene in his next comedy. His former set was jubilant about this. He was trumpeted as a good Australian. Zoë did not tell us all this on the telephone at that moment. This was pieced together later from different sources of information or misinformation.

What Zoë said, and the reason she said some of it was because she ranked Mr. Goring Hardy very high as one who both *did* and *had.* She said that to meet him was a unique chance and would be an education for a little girl like me. He thought there was promise in my book, though he did not approve of its point of view. It was possible, Zoë said, that something might come to me through his interest, but she did not want the poor little thing to be

158

hurt in any way. Goring was a fascinating fellow and he might take the imagination of a girl reared in seclusion. Too many strings had harped to his bow. Zoe's advice was that I should not be too accessible. "He wants her to call at his office at Cunningham and Bucklers, but he must meet the poor little thing in the proper way."

"I'll see to that," said Mrs Crasterton.

"I want to have her here, but I haven't a spare hour this week," said Zoe.

Mrs. Crasterton turned to me. "He must come to us. I shall let him see that you are a celebrity too."

She telephoned to the Union Club for Mr. Hardy to call her, and he did. He started by ordering that I should be sent to him — like a girl from a registry office seeking employment.

"He does feel his oats," remarked Mrs. Crasterton, aside. "But my people were bishops and generals when his were mere market gardeners."

"Oh, no," she continued into the phone. "I'm so sorry. I haven't time to go with her this week. We could try to wedge you in here though. So many people are craving for my little friend's time that the days are not long enough. Perhaps you could come to breakfast."

At last he was so generous and condescending as to say he would come to dinner that very day if we would not mind his running away immediately after. He had to open an artist's show at five and was to be at an official gathering at Government House that evening. Mrs. Crasterton said that would fit nicely as we too would be engaged until six and had an after-dinner engagement.

On that night Gaddy went to his Club. His sister asked him to support her, "After all, Mr. Hardy is a really distinguished man," she observed.

"Don't lose your head," Gaddy replied, "he certainly has marketed himself like a politician, but when it comes to literary genius, we have five hundred poets, every blooming one boomed as the greatest, but some of the greatest have yet to be born."

Derek, on the other hand, loudly lamented that he was not to be home for dinner. "Hardy's a regular swell," he said, "not in the same street with the little unwashed 'potes'."

Edmée was half through an elaborate *toilette* when we got home that evening, and poor Mrs. Crasterton was taken with cramps and had to go to bed. Edmée unselfishly gave up her dinner engagement to dine at Geebung Villa.

"It's really an amazing condescension for Goring Hardy to come to see you," she said. "It must be because Zoë de Vesey's mother knew yours and it has become the thing to see you. He is run after right and left. Some panjandrum in the literary world in London has written out to him to find out what you are like, and if you could ever write anything else. You had better make the most of your furore while it lasts."

A little later Mr. Hardy telephoned that he found himself half-an-hour ahead of his schedule and would have a chat with me before dinner. "Don't let him paralyse you," Edmée said. "Women throw themselves at him, especially the married ones . . . I think," continued Edmée reflectively, "it must be no end of sport to be safely married and then seek a little diversion."

I sat tight in my room until the maid had a colloquy with Mrs. Crasterton and then came to me. I stole down the back stairway, catching sight of my reflection in a mirror—like a doll in the white dress and Gad's big sash.

A tall figure in immaculate toggery—a dress-coat knight with silk on heel—rose from a couch and looked so hard at me that I was unable to withstand the battery of his glances. His whole face was indicative of keenness and might have been that of a money-lender, a bishop or any other manager of property and investments, instead of a poet and literary man.

The hard blue brightness of his eyes sent me firmly into my shell. He had light eyelashes that reminded me of our old white boar, whom I despised, as he did so precious little for his upkeep. Mr. Hardy's bright stare was relentless, and not free from cruelty, though I felt that he gave me swift credit for all my good points—complexion, youth, silky shining hair, feminine lines. My inventory of men was equally comprehensive and penetrating.

In thinking of him in the years that have gone I know it was his unalloyed maleness that hurt me. He would appraise women in the light of the pleasure or service they could give him. He had no scrap of that understanding for which I was hungry. That perhaps is to be found only in men of more complexity, who have something of the mothers who bore them as well as of the fathers whose name they bear.

I could be "simply ripping" to Mr. Hardy if I let fly with one side of my disposition, and there was yet another that would also be tempting to him. A man who had sipped deeply of forbidden women would like thoroughly untried soil, so I sat down primly in the full bloom of conventional innocence and waited for him to play first.

"Well, do you like Sydney?" he asked, quizzically.

"The Harbor is lovely," I breathed ecstatically.

"Well, well! You really are as young as advertised,"

161

he remarked. "I expected you to be at least thirty, with knives in your socks. Celebrities are usually well on in years before they are known."

He made remarks in the character of the fake autobiography, but that sent me as far into my shell as a winter snail, so he did a little putting to get me out again, staring with an expression of vivid interest and amusement. He was talking to one whom he estimated as without the defence of social *savoir faire*.

"How do you come to be putting up with the Old Campaigner? Is she going to see you through?"

"She is very kind to me," I rebuked him.

"She's not a bad old bolster, but you needn't feel indebted to anyone for entertaining you. You ought to charge 'em. You've provided a lot of idle resourceless women with a new sensation."

"More men than women have come to see me, and have given me luncheons and lunch parties," I said, like a child.

"By jove! Have they? I seem to be behind the times. What stamp of callers does the old Campaigner most encourage? Poets, I suppose. What would you think of a poet for a lover?"

"The Lord preserve me! Common men, when spoony, are sickly enough in poetic quotation."

"Well done, little one! I believe you could sock the balls across the net like a champion if you liked. What about Gad—the old egg, we used to call him."

"Gad is a dear," I said staunchly. "He is so kind to me."

"I expect he can't help himself." Mr. Hardy laughed shortly, with a tantalising gleam in his brilliant eyes.

Edmée appeared in her grand pale green satin with the foamy cloak half-slipping from her shoulders, and made soft coo-ing explanations of poor dear Mrs. Crasterton's indisposition. Mr. Hardy instantaneously changed into a different man, with a face as grave as a judge's and which suddenly looked lined and old. He talked in a high tenor drawl and asked if he might telephone.

While he was out, Edmée remarked, "You look all lighted up. Getting your heart cracked right at the jump?"

A little giddy, I said, "He might fall in love with me. Other men have." Roderic Quinn, Banjo Paterson, John Farrell, Rolf Boldrewood, E. J. Brady, Sidney Jephcott, Henry Lawson, Victor Daley and others had all taken notice of me in some way—some had flattered me in verses and voices of many colours, two had even kissed me—in a fraternal fashion, I ween.

"You little softy! The idea of Goring Hardy falling in love with any woman for more than a week! I heard today from old friends that it was suggested by a high official that he had better take a trip to Australia. That explains why he would waste his time here in his prime. He was much too friendly with a certain titled lady—a relative of royalty, and the husband threatened to use him as co-respondent. That bird is not to be caught with chicken feed."

We went in to dinner. Mr. Hardy made orthodox remarks with orthodox politeness, that politeness called chivalry, which women are expected to accept in lieu of their rightful control of the race and the ordering of life with sanity and justice for their children.

Mr. Hardy ignored me entirely. Edmée took it as a matter of course that he should. I was twittering internally to realise that little me from 'Possum Gully was in a SOCIETY scene at last. Here was a belle who drove men to distraction, palpitating her snowy bosom and twitching her shoulders so that no contour was wasted,

163

and languishing and ogling in the exercise of sexual attraction on a man who had been clandestinely loved by a titled married lady (there were always *clandestine* affairs in the novels of lords and ladies I had read) and wearing silk socks. I had never before seen a man wearing silk socks. My own were cashmere, and Mrs. Thrumnoddy earned money by describing them as cotton. Think of the EXPERIENCE I was imbibing in sophistication, in *savoir faire*—taking these two out of winding.

Mr. Hardy did not seem in a hurry during dinner, and acceded to Edmée's invitation to coffee before running away. He said he had telephoned, and had a half-hour longer than he expected. In the drawing-room they continued to ignore me, but I sometimes found those hard bright eyes on me in a stimulating way. Edmée gave him all sorts of gossip interesting to a homecomer. I took refuge in a big album. Here were people who by their style of dress had been old when I was born. I forgot Edmée and Mr. Hardy in wondering how many of these album people still lived, how many had gone into that awful silence, which I hate and resent.

Edmée was called to the telephone, and Mr. Hardy surprised me by springing rather than walking to my side of the room.

"Tell me what you are thinking as you look at those old frumps."

"They aren't frumps. I was thinking that once they were girls just like me, and wondering did they long for things as I do."

"Don't worry about them; they all had their day. Take yours while you can. They weren't like you: they were ordinary."

The camellia fell from his button-hole and I hastened

to replace it as Edmée returned. She laughed something about the white flower of a blameless life, and her glance had that flicker which saves her from being overlooked by the men who like women who are up in masculine sophistications, and condone them.

As Mr. Hardy was bidding good-night to Edmée he said casually, "I want your little friend to meet Cunningham the publisher tomorrow morning. I could send a cab for her".

"She will be delighted to go; it is good of you to take an interest in her," said Edmée without consulting me.

"Imagine him staying all that time—wasn't going to spare a moment at first—haw-haw, the great man!" said Edmée.

"But he went to telephone to get time immediately he saw you. Why don't you distract him?"

"What would be the use? A man of his tastes must marry money, and he's old enough in the horn to know it. But he's most fascinating."

Edmée telephoned the friends, to whom she had been going, of her triumph. Mr. Hardy had come for five minutes with the prodigy, but had stayed with her, and, as Mrs. Crasterton was ill, she could not leave the ship, and so on. Well, it was lucky when people came and saw that I was nothing, that Edmée was on hand to save them from disappointment.

The parlour maid was admitting Big Ears, so I sped to my room and left him to Edmée. I felt sure that Mr. Hardy had noticed my sash. I had not previously been noticed so intensely by sophistication, and found it thrilling. I sat down to enjoy my diary.

165

CHAPTER SEVENTEEN.

I DIDN'T SAY ANYTHING.

Mrs. Crasterton recovered on the morrow, and in the afternoon Mr. Hardy sent a cab for us and we went to meet him at the GREAT AUSTRALIAN PUBLISHER'S. People ran forward at sight of Mrs. Crasterton, and one after another conducted us through the lovely book store. Oh, the books! We went up stairs, with books everywhere, and pictures of celebrities, and entered a new kind of room to me. There were more books and pictures, but also lovely easy chairs and two desks. Goring Hardy was at one, and a terribly polite man at the other. The publisher man was away in Melbourne.

The polite man chatted to Mrs. Crasterton. Goring Hardy excused himself, something entailed cabling. Mrs. Crasterton and the Polite Man continued a conversation on family matters while I gazed about me. Oh, the books! Mrs. Crasterton had another engagement, and the Polite Man said she could leave the little lady in his charge, and he or Mr. Hardy would send her home safely in a cab. Mr. Hardy made many apologies and escorted Mrs. Crasterton down stairs with most knightly tenderness, making jokes and yarning. When he returned he dived into his papers again without taking any notice of me. The Polite Man talked to me a while and then began to shut drawers, got his stick and hat, straightened his waistcoat in the way which suggests it would be more comfortable to bone this garment unaffectedly like a bodice. Then he whispered that Mr. Hardy would soon be done, and departed.

166

Mr. Hardy, with his nose down, said that if anything urgent came in he would attend to it.

He continued quill driving until his colleague, with fussy good-byes, had withdrawn, when he flung the pen across the room to the fireplace and erected a placard with

O U T

on it, and said in an impelling tone, "Come!"

We went up a little stairway into a snuggery, which Mr. Hardy said was old Cunningham's private lair.

"What do you think of that for a chair?" said he, backing me into a huge one while he sat across the arms so that I was imprisoned. "Now, we'll enjoy ourselves."

"About writing any more books," I stammered, "I've decided not to. I shall have to earn my living. We're poor."

"We're not going to think about books today," he laughed.

"I mustn't waste your time," I said uneasily, trying to get out of the chair without touching him.

"I don't let anyone waste my time, little one. I've manoeuvred this opportunity to have a talk free from the idiots one meets at dinners and things, who want to make a tin-pot lion out of the most innocent of us."

"I couldn't possibly waste your time," I said again. I did not know how to cope with the grave breach of the conventions he was forcing upon me. I was so hurt about it that I was petrified.

"You must see these etchings," he said in a manner surprising after the way he had ignored my waiting presence for more than an hour. "Old Cunningham has some stunning prints from London, and you shall be the first to see them."

167

He went down stairs and came back with a vast book. He dawdled over every picture, but they came to an end at last and I rose again, longing to escape and murmuring about trespassing upon his time. He inquired point blank, "Don't you like being here with me? Do I bore you?"

BORED! It would have been thrilling but for the wound to my sense of propriety. He wouldn't do this to Edmée or any girl who knew the ropes, I felt.

He removed the sting by saying, "I had practically to kidnap you. There is a howling pack after you and another after me, and this was our only chance of enjoying ourselves simply. Mrs. Crasterton will know you are as safe as a church. I'll send for afternoon tea."

I sat down, but with an uneasiness which was partly genuine shyness.

"You really are more unsophisticated than I could have believed," he said, and entertained me delightfully all the afternoon. Oh, the books! I was a duck reared in a desert seeing a pond for the first time. I gained ease, Mr. Hardy was now treating me delightfully. Time ran all too quickly, and I had to insist upon departure.

"It was lovely. Thank you for entertaining me."

"Look here, we must take the law into our hands and escape to enjoy our own society, and keep it secret or we should soon be smoked out of cover. The rabble has no right to bore us to death."

This was most flattering, and he took me home to Mrs. Crasterton himself.

Edmée questioned me, but was not too persistent, as she was dressing for a ball to which Mrs. Crasterton was chaperoning her, and from which my lack both of clothes and accomplishments shut me. I said that Mr. Hardy had been too busy to bother much with me, that I had looked at a lot of books.

"But why did you stay so long?"

"I had to wait till he could bring me home."

Gaddy was to look after me for the evening, for which I was grateful in view of the danger of Big Ears turning up on the way to the ball. Gad collected children's books, which seemed to me a peculiar hobby for an old bachelor. He read from them. I never had had any children's books. Ma thought them trash and I don't believe that Pa ever heard of them.

Gad and I got on famously till half past nine, when there was a ring. "If it's Big Ears, don't leave me alone with him for a single moment," I pled.

"I promise, but why, what on earth . . . but it can wait."

It was Big Ears. In response to Gad's interrogations he said that he was bored to the spine with the dance, and why had Gad not been there?

"Why, with the beauteous Edmée, that is strange, did someone cut you out?" grinned Gad.

"Why did you neglect your duty, were you lame?" demanded Big Ears. "Derek disappeared after the first dance and left her on my hands."

"I understood that you would be after me with a gun if I did not give way," said Gad.

"Yes, and you are so persistent that the lady is worn out."

They both laughed. I listened in amazement to the workings of male vanity in saving face.

I excused myself and left Gad to the guest. He went early. One more night safely past. But I had a habit of running down to the sea wall to watch the sun rise over the Harbor, and Big Ears had found this out. There he was waiting for me next morning. He insisted upon bringing me up to the scratch. I would as soon have married a moon calf, whatever that may be, and thought it like his insufferability to be squawking after Edmée one week and trying to fool me the next, but I said I could not be so wicked as to drag him down to my level. "I'm a free-thinker," I said, piling it on a little. "It is as bad for a woman to be without religion as a flower to be without perfume. That is the companion piece of love being for men a thing apart, but for women their whole existence."

Big Ears was commended as a remarkable young man who not only taught in Sunday School, but carried on the custom of his father in reading family prayers each morning to his household. "I would laugh out loud to see you reading prayers, you'd look so funny and young," I added.

That should finish him, I thought, and raced up the terraces and into the house. Gad met me. "Hey," he began, "what about Big Ears?"

"Gaddy, I can trust you like everything, can't I?"

"That's what I'm living for," grinned he.

"Well, you see, Big Ears is trying to flirt with me, and it puts me in a fix as Edmée might think it was my fault. He is so dead gone on her."

"Did the Actem tell you that?"

"Well, yes, but you'll treat it confidentially?"

"And that put you off Big Ears—well, well, I never thought I'd be grateful to the Actem. I must give her a pair of gloves for this."

I asked what he meant, but he only cackled and kept on saying, "So she dished Big Ears by that, God bless m'soul, ha! ha!"

Mrs. Crasterton came in and wanted to hear the joke, but Gaddy winked at me and dived into his paper. Mr. Wilting's paper had come and my article was in it. I was painfully self-conscious about it, but Mrs. Crasterton praised it kindly, and I was longing for the money. I telephoned to Mr. Wilting to thank him and to ask how much I should be paid, hoping it would be enough for an evening dress.

"My dear little girl," he said, "you wouldn't get any money for that. I put it in out of my interest to keep you before the public." My acute disappointment was equalled by the feeling that I had been vulgar and pushing in bringing myself to notice. How was I to make a few shillings for an evening dress? I had suffered the notice solely to that end.

I was called to the drawing-room to meet a young man who said he was a free lance, and by interviewing me could make a guinea. I said I nearly fainted each time I was mentioned in the papers, and was trying my very best to get out of sight and be forgotten, could he not interview some important person instead? He said he would be surer of the guinea if he wrote about me, and pled with me to be a good sport and help him. He was one of a number who had come with similar pleas and who were able to make a guinea by submitting me to the torture of fresh notice, but I couldn't make a penny anywhere. The few shillings Ma had given me in pocket money were running out because people bullied me for copies of my book—said I must present one to the public library and to this and that—and I had to buy these at Cunningham and Bucklers. I felt pecked to death for lack of a few pounds. Hopes of an evening gown receded.

Mrs. Crasterton cut the interview short by calling me

to the telephone. Sir James Hobnob wanted to speak to me. I found that it was Goring Hardy. "Say," he drawled, "I enjoyed you so much yesterday that we must make a break for it again this afternoon. I'll ring the Old Campaigner again in a few minutes." He left me to do my own prevaricating.

"What did he want?" asked Mrs. Crasterton.

"He got rung off," I said

"There he is again now," she said, going to the telephone. It was Mr. Hardy saying that he was so sorry that he had been unable to give me any time yesterday— but these things can't be helped, you know. If Mrs. Crasterton would spare me again this afternoon he would see that we were not disturbed and he would advise me as best he could concerning future work. I had everything to learn. "Of course, of course," agreed Mrs. Crasterton. Today he invited me to his aunt's flat.

"Do I know your aunt?" inquired Mrs. Crasterton.

It was established that they had served together on Committees. Aunt spoke to Mrs. Crasterton on the telephone and said that she would be waiting for me at the wharf. Her flat was right in the city, which made it convenient for Goring.

Another ring was from Mrs. Thrumnoddy. She ordered me to meet her that afternoon at the Australia, where she was having a few distinguished people, and made it plain that it was a distinguished honour for me to be asked. I said I had another engagement, but she said, "Get out of it". Mr. Goring Hardy was to be with her, and a man like that had to be considered. It would do me good to meet him. Mrs. Crasterton said that I could go to her from my other engagement. I begged Mrs. Crasterton not to mention that I was seeing Mr. Hardy,

172

as it would take the wind out of Mrs. Thrumnoddy's sails, and she would put it in the paper, and Mr. Hardy would think I was a chatterer. Mrs. Crasterton said she told Mrs. Thrumnoddy only those things she wished to be reported. That settled that nicely.

Mr. Hardy himself was waiting for me at the wharf, and we jumped into a cab and went straight to his aunt's flat. Aunt looked me over piercingly, but asked no questions. Mr. Hardy spread out books and stationery in a workmanlike way and assumed his public shell towards me, which was brisk and ignoring. I dived into my rôle of girly-girly bushkin from 'Possum Gully. Presently Aunt came in hatted and with a hand portmanteau. She and Goring had a colloquy, from which I gathered that she was leaving for a week. She merely nodded good-day to me and went.

Mr. Hardy made sure that we were locked against intrusion, and then acted like a boy leaving school. He whirled me around, tossed me on to the table and sat looking at me with a leaping light in his eyes. "Now let us both come out of our shells. In spite of your cast-iron shyness there must be mines of things in you. You could not write as you do and just be the ordinary miss."

"That is just writing," I murmured.

"We cannot express passions and longings in an original and convincing way if they are not in us. It is your power of emotion that attracts me."

"My Pa put that part in for fun."

"Nonsense!" he said, and laughed. "You have a puckish sense of humour."

I said nothing, so he tried a different tack. "Do you like pretty things?"

"Oh, yes!" I exclaimed with frank eagerness. "But

173

my blue sash is the only pretty or expensive thing I have ever had, except of course, horses."

"What a dashed shame! You would be a beauty in a different sort of way if you were properly tricked out. Let me plan a turn-out from sole to crown by some smart dress-maker—something to show your curves and pretty arms."

In accordance with my upbringing it was an affront, almost an outrage to be offered clothes. Clothes could be offered with propriety only to a child or perhaps to a "person", and we were not in the person class.

"Shall we take the colour of your eyes, your hair or your cheeks and work out a scheme? I'd just like to see the flutter you would cause if you were properly dressed."

"Oh, please, my mother taught me not to accept presents from gentlemen."

"Your mother was quite right, but I am different."

"She told me that all the men would say that."

He had a real good laugh; it was nice to hear him.

"Your mother made a good job of you, but it would be quite safe to take a little present from me. It wouldn't . . . "

"It wouldn't?"

"Yes, I wouldn't—hang it all, little one, you know what I mean."

I gazed at him in owl-like fashion, which I suddenly found most effective.

"Oh, well," he said at length. "I must not expect you to run before you learn to walk in a new dimension. We must think out schemes for your future."

He asked business-like questions about my means, and I told how poor we were and that I must earn my living

174

and that I hated teaching and did not want to get married.

"Are you in love with anyone?" he demanded quite fiercely.

"Not one scrap. I never have been for a moment. I don't want ever to get married."

"That's the best poem I've heard since I left London," he laughed. "You *can* write, you know."

"Do you really think so?"

"There isn't anyone in Australia with your gifts today, but you must put them on the right rails for success. I can help you there if only we can have a little time to ourselves, without all the old cats miauling and ruining our game. You must get clear of the Old Campaigner for a start."

"She is very kind; you could come there."

"Faugh! Writers must have a retreat without anyone knowing where they are or what they are doing."

He asked me my Sydney connections, which were Pa's old-time parliamentary colleagues, especially Mr. Simms, the Minister for Education.

"We'll go and see him," said he.

I reminded him of Mrs. Thrunnoddy's tea at the Australia, where he was going, and that she had said I must go because he was to be there.

"Is that how she worked it on us? That woman would sell her skin—she hasn't any soul—to bag a social lion. Why should we go there when we can see each other here so much better?" He chuckled. So did I. "Do you think that the Old Campaigner will split about where you are?"

"No. I asked her not to because Mrs. Thrunnoddy put

175

it in the paper that I had only cotton stockings—and they are cashmere."

This made him hilarious and he put on his hat. "Come, we'll rout out a few people in Macquarie Street We must start your career."

We had a friendly time in both Houses of Parliament. I was disappointed that our law makers were such common looking old men, but to be with Mr. Hardy gave the visit glamour. Everybody made a fuss of him and seemed to think it just right for him to have me in tow. "You'll teach her the ropes and see that she makes the most of her genius," was the sort of thing they said. Mr. Hardy acted as though I were a child he was indulging, but sometimes in his eye was a look which a woman knows for what it is without EXPERIENCE. I sat on the seat beside Sir Somebody in the Upper House, and we were given tea in the M.L.A. place. Mr. Simms had us wait while he spoke in debate, and then gave us coffee in his room. I had not seen him since I was a child, and it was a day full of debate, but he was cordial and said Mrs. Simms would take me home to stay with her. Everybody thought Mr. Hardy a great man, and that my career was on the way to glory under his guidance.

He accompanied me across in the ferry. (How I revelled in travelling on the ferries!) He saw me to the gates of Geebung Villa. "We must have all the days we can together. I'll fix up something for tomorrow."

Mrs. Crasterton was quite fussy about my late appearance. She had returned a few minutes earlier to find that Mrs. Thrumnoddy had called up three times during the afternoon. Mrs. Crasterton was surprised to hear that I had not gone to the Australia. I said that Mr. Hardy had not gone either, that he thought it was much more

176

important to give me a lesson in style, and that we had been at the House of Parliament seeing my father's old friends.

Mrs. Thrumnoddy rang again. She was angry to be flouted by a little country bumpkin. Mrs. Crasterton said I had better make my own excuses. "I'm so sorry," I murmured into the 'phone, "but I was detained by the Minister for Education in Debate, and I was frightened to go to your party in *cashmere* stockings. I knew if you had Mr. Hardy I should not be missed, because he was at Parliament House while I was there, and everyone was so excited to see him that they did not notice me."

Gaddy came in while I was saying this, and patted me on the back. I told him that Mr. Wilting had not paid for my article, and Gaddy snorted, "The old swine, he wants a kick in the pants. He was too tight to turn in any copy and filled his space with your article."

There was a letter from Big Ears which thickened that plot. He said that it would be the aim of his life to turn me to spiritual things. If I would marry him, to show his tender regard, when he brought me home, prayers would be discontinued until I expressed a wish for them to be resumed. Would I meet him in the morning to give him my answer. He said he would be praying for me all night. I thought, " 'Bust him,' he ought to join the Salvation Army."

CHAPTER EIGHTEEN.

A GAME FOR TWO.

In the morning Mrs. Crasterton was again called to
the telephone by Sir James Hobnob, who asked for me.
"Dear me, poor old Sir James must be getting senile," she
remarked. "Old men can be very silly about young girls.
You must exercise common sense, my dear."

It was Mr. Hardy, chuckling. "Say, I've arranged for
you to lunch with Mrs. Simms today, and we shall have
all the afternoon together."

He rang again in a few moments in *propria persona*
and arranged the day with Mrs. Crasterton. She was busy
otherwise, and content to let me go. I went with bubbles
of anticipation inflating me.

Lunch with Mrs. Simms was mere morning tea, as that
lady was overworked opening things like bazaars to aid
poor babies or golf clubs for rich ladies, and she was
glad to be done with me. She said she would see more
of me at her house. Would I come tomorrow? She had
a big family and many friends and constituents, and some
of them were always at home. She lived at Burwood,
and a tram would take me to her door. This meeting had
been arranged by Mr. Simms and Mr. Hardy, and I was
to be left at the publishers. Mrs. Simms said I would be
wise to strike while the iron was hot.

Mr. Hardy was nearing the publishers as Mrs. Simms
deposited me on the pavement, and he saluted her very
politely. She was in a hurry, and away swung the cab.

178

Mr. Hardy, without seeming to see me, eased me off into the crowd and strode along to his Aunt's flat.

"Hooray!" he exclaimed when we were safely immured. "Another day free from the crowd."

I said no word lest I should expose my inexperience. I was a scientist with her first case, terrifically interested and as clear-headed as a cucumber. Mr. Hardy was having lunch sent in, and was free until the evening.

"Dear me," said he, sitting down and looking at me with his bright abashing gaze. "I'm back among the tall trees again with their bloom filling the world like heaven, when I look at you. To think I was once as eager and sensitive as you, ready to worship at the feet of the great! I wouldn't give up an hour with you for a week with the best girls that Sydney can bring to the post."

This would have been inebriating if real, but Ma's training was sticking to me splendidly. Was he going to "lead me astray"? It would be interesting to observe the preliminary stages. I was deprived of evening dress and dancing, but this would be something. Mr. Hardy was sympathetic about my cramped life, my desire to escape, but success, he said, had to be attacked from the jump and given no quarter. Could I stand up to the fray?

I had no more idea of what to do than a wild duck scared up from the reeds of its dam. Mr. Hardy put in that day instructing me. I must get away to London as soon as possible, while I was young and interesting. There was nothing for a person of real gifts here. I would soon be ruined if I lingered among the *local cacklers*. He used the same term as Mr. Wilting.

I timidly advanced my dream of there being an Australian soul *on its own hook,* and my desire to be part of its development. Phew! How severe Mr. Hardy was with me. That was a wicked socialistic notion which would ruin me socially and artistically. One should stick to the right crowd.

I gathered that I was well in the right crowd for a start, that I was the intimate of people who ruled the social roost, whom others—with money and position—strove to cultivate in vain. Stiff-necked egotism invaded me, for I felt it difficult to even my wits and ideas to many of the people I met, and they had B FLATS, but I did not expose my INEXPERIENCE.

I brought up the idea in a different form. Wouldn't it be self-respecting for Australian literature to do something on its own hook? This was on account of his dictum that the first thing to do was to comb the gumleaves out of my hair.

"This tosh of doing things on your own or Australia's hook, where did you get it? You want to use any hooks that come handy. The other fellows' when you get the chance: they'll use your hook if you don't look out—without saying thank you. The whole secret of success is to beat the Philistines at their own game."

I just sat and looked mousey. Even a fool is counted wise if she holds her peace.

"As for that notion of the brotherhood of man that you have, and loving the unwashed, anything in that direction is sheer drivel, drivel! Propaganda is fatal to any artist."

"What does propaganda mean?" I enquired. I knew the word only as a joke to couple with improper geese.

"Aw!" he said impatiently, "it's any of those luny ideas about the underdogs being superior because they have nothing, and the theory that their betters should support them in a velvet cage."

"I see. It's propaganda to advocate justice for the weak

180

and helpless. What is it to uphold the rich?"

"Ha! Ha!" he chuckled. "It's darned good business. It pays."

"I see," I repeated with a chill down my spine. "When you propagand for the top dogs it's not propaganda: it's like praising God: and God must be praised all the time or you'll go to hell."

Mr. Hardy laughed, but rather grimly. "See here, a man must take pride in his breed, and uphold the Empire."

"Of course, but couldn't there be different ways of upholding it?"

"Now, don't spring any more of that socialist rot about the young men's dreams, and the old men being able to rest, or you're a goner as a writer. Editors would scent you a mile off. See here, the biggest literary success, the greatest artist today is the most rousing imperialist. Gad, if only I could write like Kipling!"

To succeed by his recipe I should have to deny what I honestly felt. I should have to keep my inner self hidden from Mr. Hardy or it would be bruised and sore. What puzzled me was that my first attempt was praised for its sincerity, and yet every man who wanted to marry me or to help me in my career immediately set out to change me into something entirely different. Why not in the first place seek the writings and the girls that they wanted me to be like? There were plenty of them. No one would ever have heard of me had I not been different, but that difference was immediately to be erased.

I could not argue with Mr. Hardy. My emotions made my thought go woozy when he dragooned me both for provincialism and drivelling sentiment about the under dog. It was, oh, so easy to fall back on being a girl. That was the only side of any woman Mr. Hardy would really want

181

except those to do his cooking and laundry and other things that could be done for him equally well by men, only that he would have to pay them more.

His aunt was away for some days, and Mr. Hardy spent every one of them except Sunday with me alone. At the beginning it was a game of parry.

"Dear me," he said on the second afternoon. "It is a shame that you have no pretty things. You are meant for evening dress: you have all the lines, and flesh like pink wax. Let me see your arms."

I was shocked by this suggestion, but he insisted upon unbuttoning the simple wrist-band and turning up the bishop sleeve.

"Good gracious! and you waste your breath in admiring Edmée Actem. Her arms are drum-sticks compared with yours. To think of the scarecrows with the salt cellars under their ears and necks like a plucked fowl that are thrust upon a fellow in society, while you are covered up like a nun." He insisted that mine was the arm of an odalisque, with dainty bones and dimpled wrist and elbow.

"Any man who wasn't ossified would devour your arms," he exclaimed, proceeding to act upon his word. Then he devoured my lips until I was almost unconscious.

This was magnificently startling and thrilling and quite unexpected, that is in intensity and extent. There was something else that was intoxicating: the lightning intuition that he would not have gone as far as those devouring kisses, had I imposed restraint, even the raising of a finger. I had not invited him, being too modest for that, but neither had I exactly disinvited him.

The old wives' tales of men that filter to the most secluded girl represent men of maniacal sexual greed. I knew the gruesome tales told by midwives who have to protect their patients. The denigrating knowledge of prostitution was also known to me; there were milder confidences but always of feminine weariness opposed to merciless demands. No one had ever suggested that there would be any sensitiveness among men, that some men, however few, would, like myself, be incapable of *amour* if they were unacceptable or unless many other things such as the loved one, the time, the place and response struck twelve together.

This was a revelation of another side of the lure of the Groves of Daphne. One felt as the Ancient Mariner when he was the first that ever burst into that silent sea, for all I had heard of this previously.

Ned Crispin, Arthur Masters, Billy Olliver and others had not laid a finger on me. Was that too, male sensitiveness? I had not speculated on this before. Were men sensitive only in the presence of virginity? Once the bar was down did they lose all respect? It did not seem that I could ever find a man with whom I could retain my self-respect in such a surrender.

Mr. Hardy and I were at variance on my deeper and inner ideas, but in playing the most magic game known we were equally matched in this vein of sensitiveness. I was his quarry because of my inexperience, but he was equally mine in my thirst for knowledge.

I was so elated by the discovery that maidenly safety lay in my own hands that I planned some sorties on my own account. This arrangement of going to Mrs. Simms acted admirably for liberty. It was another inebriating thing to discover that in a great city one could have adventures and no one the wiser. In the bush the very crows and magpies reported every movement. Little wonder that city people were wickeder than those in the bush, with opportunities and temptations so available.

I decided to go secretly to the *Bulletin* office. The *Bulletin* was a mine of fascination, but not considered nice for young girls or clergymen. I had a friend in its office, Mr. A. G. Stephens. I was much more eager to know him than dozens of silly old Sir James Hobnobs and stuffy professors and ponderous parliamentarians, but Mr. Stephens was regarded as a devil with horns. I asked was he a liar or a thief or a rake, and the reply always was, "Oh, no, not that, but the man is *wrong-headed.*" By persistent cross-examination I elicited that he discussed sympathetically the works of men who promulgated abashing views on sex and sociology: someone named G. B. Shaw, in particular. I sounded Mr. Hardy about him, and it was laughable to hear his execration of a real hog who would subvert society. As for my meeting "that crowd", well, that would be to throw pearls of innocence before the swine of dangerous propaganda.

Nothing could now have stopped me from going to Mr. Stephens, and I climbed to his office and spontaneously burst into affection for him in a fraternal and intellectual way. How generous he was! He took me to tea, he gave me books, wonderful new books for my own that I had not dreamed of possessing. He talked in a whimsical way with twinkles in his eyes, adding to my literary education in every paragraph.

He asked about my future work, and was it true that Mr. Hardy had me in hand? "Would you advise me to make a model of Mr. Hardy?" It was as funny as a circus to hear his views of Mr Hardy. He did not exhibit the vehemence against Mr. Hardy that Mr. Hardy had against Mr. Stephens, but was equally damning. I should not think of such a man at all. His work was thin and vicious, imitative; he had been unable to work in Australian material, so had decamped to London and there echoed a cheap kind of smartness. It would be suicidal for me to ape such a course. Hardy lacked literary or any other ideals.

If some fairy had offered me a gift I should have chosen to be able to draw, so I asked breathlessly for Norman Lindsay. He was young like myself, his drawings were more shocking than my book, and he was equally talked about. Mr. Stephens shook his head. Norman would not be interested in me: I was not his type physically or mentally. He would be contemptuous of me as a bread and butter miss. No coaxing would make him disgorge Norman, but he gave me a book illustrated by him.

Mr. Stephens sent a messenger to Geebung Villa with the parcel of books, but I would not let the Norman Lindsay drawings out of my possession and departed on the adorable little King Street cable tram with them clasped to my bosom. I was to lunch with Zoë de Vesey at Potts Point, and I burst in with the drawings in triumph. Mr. Hardy was also there for lunch. Zoë did not bag social lions: people knew they were in SOCIETY if she noticed them, and so sought her invitations. With opportunity they turned from lions into tame house cats for ever under her feet.

I gurgled inwardly to hear Mr. Hardy fulminate about those drawings. He said to Greville de Vesey that it showed what kind of a swine the fellow was to give such things to a child like Sybylla. Zoë said, "Nonsense! I am so glad, Sybylla, that Mr. Stephens gave you those drawings. I must ask him to lunch. If I had a daughter I would much rather give her Lindsay's drawings than let her read that sloppy trash of the Greatest Australian

Writer for Girls—it is enough to bemuse girls mentally and morally."

Mr. Hardy wanted to take the Lindsay book from me, but I put it safely on Zoë's bed. I was looking forward to showing the drawings to Great-aunt Jane.

After lunch I got Zoë aside and said as she knew all about SOCIETY and LIFE and LOVE would she tell me how the fascinating belles managed to refuse to marry men and retain them for QUONDAM LOVERS. I was ambitious for such possessions. "That's the ABC. . You must make each man feel that he has broken your heart, and but for some fluke you would have married him. That works like a charm, but of course it requires a little finesse."

Four o'clock found Mr. Hardy and me together again in the flat. He may have been as great a rake as reported, who thought no more of cracking a woman's heart than of shooting a partridge, a man of the London world, a society idol who had achieved money and réclame by comedies of sultry duchesses and adulterous clubmen—Piccadilly club-men—but with me he was an Australian and kept to Australian rules in the game.

"Such innocence! Such inconceivable innocence!" he would exclaim. "I should like to take you away and shut you up somewhere so that your quaint childish purity would never be spoiled, and keep you for myself."

I *was* innocent. I had only intuition to guide me, but suddenly woman's knowledge had come and I was ages old in rebellion, and I did not kindle because I felt that Mr. Hardy looked on women as being created solely for the delight of men. I often chuckled to myself to picture how incredulous Zoë or Edmée would have been that Goring Hardy found me sufficient entertainment for hours to-

186

gether. Zoë would have thought me on the high road to having my unseasoned heart cracked. She would not have guessed that I was offsetting exploitation of unsophistication by turning *amour* inside out to see the wheels of passion go round.

A fool is counted wise if he holds his peace, can be made to work by a woman if she is young and her eyelashes are long. Whirlwinds of sophistication won't protect a man from gullibility in this respect. A woman has the advantage if she is equally matched in intelligence. To start, a man is an open book to her while she has depths that he does not suspect because some of them he will not concede to her. He insists that they are not natural for a woman, and it being impossible to fully cheat nature he only cheats himself.

Goring Hardy would sit in a big chair and pull me to his knee. Oh, Aunt Jane and Ma if only you had seen that I could sit there without danger to my virtue, because that issue lay in my own hands! Dangerous—perhaps. So was it to ride a rampant stallion in girl-girly skirts, but approximately safe with skill. I had come to like the kisses, but any further caress or familiarity waited on a release which I did not give. Automatically any infringement of my code would have sent me up and away startled and resentful, and Goring Hardy was sensitively aware of that.

As he revelled in my innocence I grew more and more unsophisticated before his eyes. This was easy because I was genuinely blindfolded by INEXPERIENCE. Simple silence or to hang my head when in doubt had the desired result. I sat muffled in modesty: there was no chink through which a breeze of illicit *amour* could make its way. He would ask me what I was thinking. I withheld that I was pondering the monotony of such procedure, which could lead to nothing but consummation, and that was out of the question to me. Then, would there come only monotony and satiety again? Disillusion. Must one become drunk to find rapture in *amour,* or remain without illusion? It appeared so from what evidence I could garner, and that was a fatiguing thought to me.

If, in trying to usurp the maternal rights of the race as well as their own, men have accentuated the simple eternal feminine until it is cloying and infernal, no less have they made over-virilised masculinity equally infernal, crude and repellent.

"Haven't you any feeling? Are you made of ice? Are you anything of a woman or are you only a spirit?" he would demand, kissing my arm. I watched the aforesaid wheels turning, my innocence outwardly intensifying, quietly, easily self-contained. My attitude and very tone of voice had been ingrafted by generations of conventionalised, continent mothers who had swallowed the prescriptions laid down for them by men instead of developing themselves in the exercise of natural law, and with nothing to ease their lot but the superstition that the impositions foisted upon them had been God's will.

He would sometimes lay out a fairy tale. I was to go to London and have a retreat where he and I would work. How baffled I felt by INEXPERIENCE. It bound me like a cocoon. I imagined how Edmée would revel in like case, how histrionically she would handle it. All Sydney would know that Goring Hardy had been madly in love with her, that he had kidnapped her and shut her up with him while hostesses had been expecting them and suffering the ruin of parties by their absence. Everyone would know that her heart too had been just a little touched, and she would achieve glamour.

Whereas I did not get the enjoyment to which I was entitled because I did not know how to handle the situation and feared that Goring Hardy was regarding me as he might have a chorus girl or a social inferior who would be on all fours by his patronage. However, when you don't know what to do, do nothing. If a young woman in her teens wishes to pile on innocence one of the surest recipes is to murmur something about MOTHER. I said I did not think my mother would let me go to London. That shooed him off those suggestions.

"I wish to God I could marry you," he would say vehemently, "but I can't afford to." He would be imploring, heated and almost angry by turns at what he called my iciness.

"I cannot marry you, but by jove, how I wish I could," he would repeat, speaking as if to marry me he would only have to ask. I might have succumbed if he had invited me inside a wedding ring, but I knew, young and inexperienced though I was, that it would never work, and no man living could have tempted me outside a wedding ring. I had been so reared that any other suggestion was so deadly an insult that it iced any emotion I might have had.

On one occasion when he repeated his refrain I murmured, "Perhaps it would not make anyone happy to marry you. Someone told me you are a terrible flirt."

"The Old Campaigner, I suppose," he sneered.

"No, she thinks you a very distinguished man."

"Then, who was it?"

"It's in the air, from all the society women; they say you are a rake."

He flared into sentiments ignoble before an unsophisticated girl, so defenceless that he could say, "I'm sorry. I can't marry you," to her face without fear of being snubbed.

He said women were a pack of cats, only that was a politer word than he used. I said nothing at all. When the first fury passed he said women had no call to talk about men, that a woman's whole aim in life was to chase some poor devil and trap him into having to slave for her for ever after.

I thought this cowardly inconsistency seeing that women were compelled to marry by nearly all other occupations being closed to them, and by the pressure of public opinion. Men want it both ways like a bully arranging a game.

Mr. Hardy continued that there wasn't one woman of all the pack, who, if she had the chance without being found out, would not have taken a swifter gait than he had, and that it was typical of feminine treachery for them to betray him to me; but I thought it loyal on their part to warn me.

"What did you say to those low cats?" he demanded.

"Nothing at all. I thought I'd wait for your defence."

At that he smiled wryly. "If you were an ordinary girl, I could make a defence, but all the things that satisfy other girls, seem to lose their value when offered to you."

So this was an example of an uncrude man making love. He had been an artist in beating up his game. It may have been demoralising to the game, but perhaps EXPERIENCE cannot be harvested without some demoralisation. AUNT'S holiday was nearly done and I had my worries, so I said plaintively, "Are you sure that you couldn't marry me—aren't you rich enough at all?"

"It's quite out of the question, little one. We must

both marry money. Love in a garret and sacrificing one's self for the lower orders is delirium tremens. The common people are not worth lifting and are the first to turn on those who waste their talents in trying to better the world."

It seemed to me that it was not merely a matter of lifting the helpless, but that certain people could not find oil for the soul in them if they did not give ear to the still small voice of justice and fair play.

"Then I must go away and not see you any more for I don't want to be so terribly hurt that I can't bear it," I murmured, applying Zoë's recipe, to which I clung dumbly, refusing to explain or to add or subtract a syllable.

And that was the end of that little bit of psychological research.

CHAPTER NINETEEN.

IN NEED OF A FRIEND.

There was a dismal letter from home awaiting me at Geebung Villa. Pa's sciatica, Ma's rheumatism, the rain gauge and every sign combined could not bring rain to the Southern District. It was in a ghastly state. Even the curlews were puzzled and the new moon unreliable. The rabbits, however, flourished unabatingly. Pa had been laying phosphorus baits and had got too many whiffs and was not well. Ma said I was needed at home to look after things.

It was time for me to go in any case. Otherwise I should lose my excursion ticket, and we had no money for an extra fare. I wrote to catch the mail to 'Possum Gully, stating when I should be in Goulburn. I had two more days in Sydney.

There was also a letter from Big Ears telling me he was going over the Gap if I continued to spurn his undying love. This scared me stiff. There would be a dreadful scandal. I should be regarded as a murderer, and no one would have any sympathy for a girl so unsexed as to write books. I could not handle this alone. Mrs. Crasterton would not quite understand. I longed for a friend. Edmee was no good in that respect except for me to admire. It was all on my side. Her vanity would be upset that Big Ears had transferred his aberration. She might blame me for being underhand. I shrank from Derek's ridicule. Zoë, I felt, would be a tower of strength, but she had gone to Brisbane for a holiday.

Dear old Gaddy! He would understand. He would not lecture me about the way I did not want to go. I was ashamed that I had not appreciated Gaddy until this moment. He had given the blue sash in such a way that I could accept it. He had "shouted" all the plays and concerts that I had seen. Like Sister Anne on the parapet, or wherever she took up her stance, I had been looking for a knightly lover and had disregarded Gaddy because he had a double-chin and a girth like the mayor-and-corporation, and breathed so that I could always hear him if the conversation died down a little. He could not be idealised as a lover, but there had been more pestiferation than pleasure in lovers as known to me; and Gaddy's person was formed to buttress friendship. I was famishing for a friend. When all is said and done, friendship is the only trustworthy fabric of the affections. So-called LOVE is a delirious inhuman state of mind: when hot it substitutes indulgence for fair play; when cold it is cruel, but friendship is warmth in cold, firm ground in a bog.

"Gaddy, come into the garden with me, like Maud," I pled. "I love it and the Harbor so, but I'm not safe there without you."

Gaddy always did what he was asked without fuss, and no one noticed how unselfish he was because he was fat and old. He waddled around the flower beds plucking me a masculine bouquet—a leafless mixture of bloom, short of stalks and tightly compressed, but it smelt of heaven.

I confessed my trouble with Big Ears, and Gaddy wanted to know could I not consider him. I said I'd rather earn my living as a nurse maid. "Well, then," said Gaddy, "just don't bother about him."

193

"But supposing he should commit suicide!"

"I'll tell Derek, he'll knock sense into him."

This brought relief mixed with fear of Derek's ridicule. I then told Gaddy about the drought and Pa being ill, and that I had to go home. Gaddy said that that was no sort of a career for a girl like me. I said my literary career had entirely gone bung in Sydney. Gaddy wanted to know what this fellow Hardy had been doing to help me. "Is he putting you in a play or what? A fellow like that doesn't waste his time without getting something out of it."

"What do you mean?"

"Oh, a little bird told me that a certain AUNT was away."

So it seemed there were crows and magpies in Sydney as well as in the bush. "He wanted me to turn into someone that I am not, and go to London, but we have no money for that."

Gaddy snorted and walked about a bit. "It's a shame," he said. "You need a patron, who would let you be yourself, and then you would have a brilliant career. Or you should have some cushy job with plenty of cash and leisure; but those jobs are given to men with influence. It would never do to let women have them, or where would men get wives?" He said this with a grin which extracted the sting.

Things would be righted now that women had the vote, but it would not be in time to help me, and I had not the necessary education. Gaddy breathed around the drive a bit and then we sat on the sea wall and he said, "There is a way that it could be settled as tight as a trivet."

"Tell me how?" I demanded eagerly. Gaddy looked

strange, even apoplectic, and his eyes bulged as if he were twisting his squint straight to look at me.

When a woman has warning she can obviate the conventional fable that a man stutters or mutters about loving her more than life or a good dinner, and which necessitates the companion fibs about being unworthy of his love combined with humble thanks for the honour he has offered her in the opportunity to be his wife, likewise drudge, echo, unfailing flatterer and so on. I had no warning from Gaddy. He said that I needed time and leisure to develop my kind of genius, and as he had plenty of money for the job, and loved me better than all the flash and selfish exploiters of my youth and beauty put together were capable of doing, what about solving my problem and making him as proud and happy as a pup with two tails by becoming Mrs. Gad.

It was a disgracefully crude thing to have done, but I put my fingers in my ears and fled to my room. No firm ground anywhere. "Oh, Gaddy, Gad!" I said in my grief. "How could you betray me so? How could you?" To lean on FRIENDSHIP and find treacherous AMOUR in its sheep's wool! Old Grayling and Henry Beauchamp at 'Possum Gully, and Big Ears and Gaddy in Sydney. My career had certainly gone bung at both ends and in the middle. Kerplunk! Bang!

I sat in the dusk and suffered my plight. Mrs. Crasterton might think that I had led her brother astray. I folded the blue sash and put it on Gaddy's desk and continued to sit in the dark. I had recently read an article about men with gooseberry eyes and big girths making splendid husbands, but that girls passed them over to throw themselves under the feet of the man who would make their lives a misery because he could grace a dress suit and top hat. Gad and Goring. Goring had none of Gad's unselfish generosity. Gaddy might even be noble, yet so powerful is appearance that the phrases of AMOUR would have GLAMOUR from Goring while Gaddy was so fat that his protestations could be nothing but fatuous. Such are the stupid tricks that NATURE plays. I wonder why.

It was Mrs. Crasterton's At Home night. Wheeler coiffured the ladies. I heard Gaddy come in and dress across the corridor. Derek called to his mother, "Who's coming tonight?"

She named three members of the Cabinet, a university professor of note, an editor, several social nonentities, and the Chief Justice.

"The usual rabble," said Derek, "but I might look in to see the Chief." Derek was designed for something brilliant in the law.

"That will be nice, darling," cooed his mother. I sat and shrank and shrank in the dark and wished I were back at 'Possum Gully. I was misplaced in SOCIETY. Think how Edmée carried off admirers! They all made a fool of me, but think how she made fools of them so that they were for ever muttering around town about her, and trying to make out that she pursued them.

I was worried about Big Ears, as no doubt Gaddy would now leave him on my hands.

Everybody went down. There was great asking where was I, and at length Mrs. Crasterton came and turned on the light and found me. I felt a terrible fool. I said everything had gone wrong. Poor old Pa was not well, and the drought terrible, and it was wicked to be in Sydney enjoying myself while Ma had been struggling at home. I was as bad as a man who went on the spree. I said that I had written of my departure.

Mrs. Crasterton was kind and consoling. I pled to go to bed, but she said that would be no way to get the best out of the opportunities that Ma had let me have, that I must come down and put my worries aside. Only amateurs of life let their set-backs be known. "I'll send Wheeler to tie the sash. She is an artist with bows."

I said if I appeared in the sash again it would seem as if I went to bed in it. Mrs. Crasterton said that helped my quaintness.

I had to go down to dinner. Gaddy ate a large meal. He did not seem to be abashed or upset, whereas my food stuck in my throat. "The old toad, to spoil friendship," I kept thinking to myself. "The old toad!"

Derek was an exposition of style from his patent leather toes to his shining hair. He gurgled and chuckled and winked at me until I did not know which way to look. At least it seemed that Big Ears couldn't be in danger of *felo de se*.

Derek took me aside at the end of dinner and said that he had taken up my case with Big Ears. "He must be given a penny and told to take his hurdy-gurdy to some other corner. We don't like the noise here."

"You won't let him commit suicide?"

Derek laughed. "People with his make of ears never die for love. They propose to all the girls and at last one takes them and they rear a big family and praise God."

Mrs. Crasterton here summoned him. The Chief Justice had come early to have a few words with me. Derek surprised me by presenting me to the lovely old man with a beautiful mop of white hair. "They've all tried to spoil her, but she's full of wit and common sense and takes everyone out of winding. She's the richest thing I ever

197

met. Her judgments of people would amuse you, Sir."

Derek beamed upon me every now and again. Gaddy actually shone with feats of interestingness and attentiveness to all and sundry. A couple of lieutenants from the Flagship engaged Edmée's attention. They were so carried away by her that they wound up like a clock stopping when Mrs. Crasterton tried to put them in circulation. She remarked afterwards that so many young Englishmen reminded her of underdone suet dumplings.

A cabled item in the evening papers was discussed. A certain nobleman was suing for divorce from his wife and naming as co-respondent an officer of the Guards. It was infatuation for this lady, said the quid nuncs, which had resulted in Goring Hardy coming to Australia and remaining so long. He would be now free to return to London. They speculated whether or not he would marry Lady Hartlepool when she should be free, whether he had been writing during his visit or if his time had been entirely wasted. "Was there no Sydney young lady able to engage his fancy?" inquired Sir James Hobnob, making eyes at Edmée. She languished and got away splendidly with the suggestion that she had not exerted herself, that he was much, much too old for her.

"A fascinating chap," brayed Sir James. "A real man of the world, and a great name in Australian literature."

"You bet," said Derek. "The only Australian literary name that cuts any figure on a cheque."

To my consternation Big Ears was announced. He soon found his way to me and concentrated his gaze upon me until I thought I should go off into yelps of nervous laughter. The Lord be praised, Edmée came to the rescue. She needed someone to set against the naval boys, and Big Ears was the nearest insect.

198

"That's what I call a wind in your favour," said Derek, as he slipped into a seat beside me. "What's this about you leaving us so soon? I had planned all sorts of things for you next week."

"I should have been here next week," I murmured. Then he said I was the jolliest little chum who had been in the house for ages. "All sorts of freaks impose on the Mater, but I have felt that perhaps she imposed on you, letting you carry all this social blither without any armour, so to speak."

I had heard him making fun of my lack of wardrobe and my unsophisticatedness. "I've felt that I was chasing you from home," I said.

"I always go out as much as possible when Edmée comes to stay. She'd jolly well have me up for breach of promise, if I wasn't too slippery. I warn Gaddy to put nothing in writing. I'm sick of her family too. It's all a fellow can do to put up with the breadth and antiquity of his own without having someone else's mouldy pedigree thrust down his throat with the breakfast bacon and dinner soup."

"Oh, but I think Edmée is lovely."

"So does she, but all but herself recover from the delusion in time. If she doesn't soon hook a fish she'll be *passée*. Let's tackle Big Ears together. I'll be best man if you like."

This was too much of a finish on the day and I could not keep my lips from quivering. "I'm sorry," he said quickly. "I'll take the beastly little green-grocer out the back and we'll give him the order of the turnip."

He beckoned to Big Ears and extracted me quietly through the hind door and took us upstairs to his own snuggery. I said I wanted to return safely into his own

199

hands the lovely jewellery that Big Ears had so kindly lent me, as I was going home.

"And I've just been telling her not to take any notice of you," chirped Derek, "that you are such a devil of a fellow with the girls, you have half-a-dozen on the string at once. Sybylla is as serious as a pest, so I hope you have not been flirting with her."

Derek was an audacious wag. I left the situation to him. He represented me as too young and simple to be pestiferated with the confisticated boredom of marriage. "Why, even I would not dare to flirt with Sybylla. I'm letting her mature unmolested. I love her as a sister, but no larks with such a clever young lady." If only he had flirted with me just a little, how delightful it would have been. He was so full of fun that he amused everyone. People always helped him laugh, but anyone who attempted to laugh at him came a cropper.

"You wait till she comes to town a year hence," advised Derek. "And what's more, my beauty, you're going into training for our tennis tournament. I mean to make a champion of you."

"A champion at paying all the loose ends of expenses," murmured Big Ears.

"Well, you'll have your portrait painted for that as soon as you get a tummy to fill the middle of a canvas. When training, the first rule is that you must not think of a lady. Nothing so puts a man out of condition."

"That's pugilists," protested Big Ears.

"What will put the punch into pugilists is good enough to give a forehand wallop to your serving. Now, assure Sybylla that she mustn't have any spoony drivel for a whole year at least. You are as free as air. So is she. In a year's time, we shall see."

I gave Big Ears his bracelets. He began to discuss the possibility of getting into a first-class game, and we three returned to the drawing-room together.

The people dribbled away rather early that night. The Editor stopped a moment on the doormat talking to Mrs. Crasterton and promised to ring up in the morning.

Gad insisted upon my having a talk with him in his study as I went up to retire. I did not feel too easy, but did not know how to escape.

"Dear, dear," said Gaddy, "so you have returned the sash like a novelette. You take life too hard altogether. Cuss it, I don't think it will hurt either of us for you to keep that piece of rag. So my little bit of spoof scared you! I did not understand what an inexperienced child you are. I'm awfully sorry that I upset you, because I have no other feeling but one of friendship."

Waves of shame swept all over me to find what a fool I had made of myself, but I was learning the technique of dissimulation hour by hour. If only I had kept my head and applied Zoë's recipe!

"Oh, Gaddy, I really thought for a moment that you were in earnest, because others have been, you know, or thought they were for an hour or two, and you were such a lovely friend that it was sad to have you turn spoony."

"That's what we are always going to be, I hope— friends."

On this note we separated, I with the sash in my hand.

I had a tortured sleepless night. I roamed into Edmée's room. She was sleeping as soundly as Mrs. Crasterton, and as audibly. All the lovers raging for Edmée or misconstruing her actions did not agitate her. A beauty, no doubt, early grows accustomed to that sort of thing. I envied Edmée her royal self-satisfaction. She had been

201

adulated all her life so that her ears caught only approval, while mine, supersensitive and directed to concentrate on shortcomings, accumulated and retained only wounds and let the plaudits go.

I was disturbed by the antics of Big Ears and by Derek's intervention; and Gad's case was more botched-up than happily erased. I could not be sure that he had been joking. Even had he been, the worry was merely transferred to my being the fool. Derek too added to my humiliation by emphasising his brotherliness. Did I appear to him as absurd as a figure of romance as Gaddy did to me? Could I have had just one evening dress and dancing lessons I could have had some fun among people of my own age.

I should be relieved to escape to 'Possum Gully and leave my measley little pig-dog career behind me in Sydney.

CHAPTER TWENTY.

IT MIGHT *Not* HAVE BEEN.

I breakfasted early to escape the embarrassment of Gaddy's presence. I ran down to the sea wall and, to my surprise, saw Derek and Big Ears disporting themselves in the/shark-proof enclosure. Derek's dazzling teeth appeared in a gay smile. He had evidently begun training— was really a friend in shouldering the job of curing Big Ears.

During the forenoon Mrs. Crasterton, Mrs. Simms and the Editor of the previous evening were in telephonic communication. Then Mrs. Crasterton asked me how I would like to remain in Sydney and do the WOMAN'S LETTER on one of the big newspapers. The present writer under the alias of Lady Jane, was paid seven pounds a week, but of course I could only be offered half that as a beginning. Even so, it seemed an enormous amount of money to have each week. Little me who never had a penny, at any rate not five pounds spent on me in a whole year! It was a dazzling prospect until I picked it to pieces.

What would I have to write? I should have to lackey around to all the SOCIETY affairs and describe Lady Hobnob's dresses and Sir James's wonderful cellar—in short kow-tow to a lot of people who had not advanced my search for something better than 'Possum Gully. Quite the contrary: they were disappointing results of the opportunities for which I was avid. What was the present Lady

Jane going to do? This was rather glozed over. She had been growing duller and duller. I would go around with her for a month to learn the ropes. But what would she do then? That was her problem, not mine, I was told. "But she would hate me for taking her position from her!"

"My dear, you'll never be a success in society or the professions unless you are indifferent about hate or love. It's a sign of your own worth sometimes if you are hated by the right people."

That scared me off entirely. How could I take another woman's livelihood from her? I would rather share what I had with her. It was described as a tragedy that I, with my talents, should return to feeding the pigs and milking the cows, and white-washing hearths and shining pot-lids—a poverty-stricken grind in a petty domesticity which I hated. Mrs. Simms said that nevertheless she was glad that I did not attempt the journalistic job, which for women of any mental capacity was so devitalising—writing rot about recipes and ball-dresses and becoming a disheartened and frustrated hack. I was so young yet, there was time for literary talent to develop. Writing was not, as some vocations, dependent upon youth. And that was that.

The glorious escape from 'Possum Gully, or what was to have been a glorious escape, had ended in nothing but a wish to return to 'Possum Gully as an escape from the escape that was not glorious.

That was a painfully flat day. Mrs. Crasterton had made arrangements exclusive of me, as for the past week I had been *on my own hook*. Edmée had gone to a garden party. I arranged my belongings ready for flight. Life seemed to have run aground. The Harbor was divine

204

in the full day sun, brilliant blue but with a breath of haze like a veil, and little grey cow tracks all across it like sashes on the tides. The small waves whispered of the tides on the rocks covered with oyster shells and draped in seaweed with a grand sedgy odour. The gulls rocked about like paper boats at play. Out beyond the Heads the swelling Pacific towered high as a plain. Behind was the city so full of people, but nowhere in it had I found anyone to whom I could tell my perplexities with any hope of being understood or really helped. They would criticise and advise, but Ma and Great-aunt Jane had already furnished me with that kind of friendship and assistance.

I sat on the sea wall and looked down at the jetty at Pannikin Point. We always came home to Geebung Villa that way when we had no luggage needing a cab. Gaddy got off the ferry boat in company with a tall man. Gaddy added to the friction in my thoughts, so I stayed on the terrace with the camellias and watched the shipping. Presently he approached, calling me. When he appeared before me he flung out a leg and waltzed, an indulgence for aesthetic reasons improper to a corpulent man.

"Do you know who has put off his departure a whole day on purpose to see you—enough to give you swelled head, young woman. He heard about you on arrival, put in last night reading your book—guess who it is."

"It couldn't be Renfrew Haddington!"

"The very man! My idea of a real man and a literary josser combined—very rare, for I largely agree with old Wilting about local cacklers."

Here was the really truly GREATEST AUSTRALIAN POET, but when a man had so many other distinctions it was easy to overlook this trifling indigenous dementia. He was known as one of the really influential journalists on the Australian press. He had represented the *Melbourne Tribune* in the Boer War. His despatches had been so sound that they had also been snapped up by London and American journals. His book on the war was considered a masterpiece alike by those who thought the war ignoble and by the swashbucklers. He had been lecturing in the United States and was on his way home.

Gad reminded me of all this, but I was not excited. I was subdued by campaign bruises. EXPERIENCE was teaching me that people sought me for their own entertainment, not for mine, and that those supposed to be interesting were frequently less so than those reported to be otherwise.

I had to return to the house with Gad, feeling insignificant and crest-fallen, but I did not care. This was my last night in Sydney. Pa and Ma had not been to Sydney for more than ten years, and as far as I could see it might be all that before I could come again.

Mr. Haddington came across the lawn to meet me as I kept behind Gaddy. He was tall and broad and brown, and there was something restful and enfolding about him so that I ceased to be driven to act any role whatsoever.

I drank of his understanding as I looked into his deep kind eyes, and gained assurance as he looked deeply back into mine. The world lit up with new possibilities. I was glad that Renfrew Haddington was alive and there holding me by the hand. I was refilled with the false hope of youth that happiness could come to me some day with shining face as a prince or knight and that a struggle to remain available for such an advent was worth while.

Manliness seemed to emanate from the man, with patience and strength as well as kindliness. He had bumpy features and iron grey hair, and no superfluous flesh. The eyes looked searchingly from cavernous sockets with an illumination of spirit which he could impart. Most men are so elemental that I suffocate in my antiquity of spirit by comparison, but Mr. Haddington suddenly made me feel young and overcoming as if the awful things in life could be reformed. Here was a soul and mind in which one could take refuge.

I do not remember saying much to him, yet I felt that he knew a better self of me than consciously existed. He was departing on the Melbourne Express, and could not stay to dinner.

"Men will always seek you for your sympathy and understanding," he said, as he held my hand in parting.

I was late down to dinner, and as I came in, Edmée was discussing the recent caller in her own style, and impressed upon me that I had been highly honoured. "What do you think of him?" she asked for the third time.

"I like him better than any human being I ever met," I said, just like that.

"The doll awakes from petrifaction," laughed Edmée. "We must get his son over from Melbourne. He must be as old as you."

"I have never met Mrs. Haddington," remarked Mrs. Crasterton.

"She's a remarkably fine woman," said Gaddy. "She needs to be to measure up to Haddington."

I excused myself early. I wanted to write notes of good-bye to be posted on the morrow, but instead I sat recalling how Mr. Haddington had looked as he stood talking to Gad on the lawn in the light of the setting sun while I watched him from the drawing-room window curtains. I examined the inscription in the book he had given me. Magical that his hand had written there for me, the product of his own brain. If such a man was honoured because he wrote books, surely the attempt was not unvaliant for an ignorant girl. Surely none but piffling people thought that girls should not write. Renfrew Haddington would not think so. There must be numbers of similar men in the world. I had met few because I knew so few of all kinds, and humanity in the aggregate is so chock-a-block with culls.

When the household retired I continued to sit by my window looking at the twinkling lights of the city, lovely, alluring: they should have held something much nobler than I had met.

Why had Mr. Haddington stirred me so? I couldn't be in love at first sight with a man old enough to be my father—that would be disgusting; but why should he be able to give a different meaning to life?

As many as a dozen old men have tried to probe if there was a real Harold Beecham to correspond to the hero in my book, and when I assure them that Harold Beecham was made out of imagination they still cling to their own notion. Many young men have told me that they *are* Harold Beecham or intend to be: girls ask is it true that Harold Beecham was drawn from their suitors because the suitors are claiming so to give themselves added weight and attraction. HAROLD BEECHAM! Pooh, he was the best I had been equipped to imagine at the time. Mr. Haddington had given me an idea of something much better furnished. Now I could see what Mr. Wilting and others meant when they said I had been too inexperienced to attempt a love scene. Mr. Hardy at one end of the scale and Mr. Haddington at the other had been a revelation.

I fell all night from spoke to spoke of a mental wheel:
His son is as old as you are.

His wife is a mighty fine woman.

I am the merest of women and the most special cannot marry where they list.

The one man of our dreams would be sure to rush into marriage early.

Nothing matters.

So what does it matter after all?

Pa always says it will be all the same in a hundred years.

A hundred days, a hundred months are a long dull stretch when taken piecemeal.

His wife is a remarkably fine woman.

This at any rate was something to be thankful for. If a man with the power to so impress me had been such a driveller as to yoke with a nincompoop or a "tart", I should have felt disgraced.

The following night I fell from spoke to spoke of a different wheel—that of the gallant steam engine which tugged the mails and passengers from Sydney to Melbourne.

Despite an arid interior my last day in Sydney was a heavenly specimen of weather—blue and gold—the Harbor lovelier than a dream. Every garden in the roomy suburbs sprawling on the city's ridges gave forth a wealth of roses and semi-tropic bloom. The thoroughfares were decorated with comely young people in white and gay colours. The city piles were outlined against the effulgent sunset ocean of liquid gold as I returned to Geebung Villa for the last time. The misty bays were a fairyland of twinkling lights as we crossed in the ferry and took a cab to Redfern.

Mrs. Crasterton was horrified that I should be travelling second class, but as in the matter of dresses she did not let it run to her pocket. "All those dreadful, coarse men," she whispered, "Are you sure you will be safe with them? They look like working men."

That's what they were—station hands—and I felt as safe with them as with a gum tree. "We won't be out of Sydney before they will be doing everything for me."

She gave me a final hug and thanked me for my visit, which she said had brought so many old friends around her and so many new ones that she was quite rejuvenated.

The men, who were shearers, disposed of my luggage and gave me my choice of a seat, just as I expected, and I leaned from the window to draw a breath from the luxuriant gardens of Strathfield, where the lights were putting out the starry evening.

The men talked of the drought and the terrible plight of the land immediately beyond the coastal belt, but the present hour was redeemed by moonlight. Moonlight is as lovely and as thrilling as a phantom. The silver glory etherealises the grimmest landscape. Soon it transformed the drought and filled the wide night universe with mystery and enchantment.

Scent of wattle drifted in from Liverpool onward. The good engine roared and tugged, shaking the tiny houses of fettlers beside the line, on, and on, through the potency of the wide and silent but echoing night. Not a month since I had left the bush, but EXPERIENCE had made it a cycle.

Otherwise I was taking nothing back from the city but a blue sash and the books given to me by Mr. Stephens. I was clearly not a getter. Financially, I was as helpless as Pa. But my retreat was only a withdrawal. I would come again. I must start again from the beginning. I must stick to myself henceforth. I must go beyond Sydney. Few of the people I had met in Sydney had anything more in them basically than those around 'Possum Gully. The difference was in their having and doing, not in their *being*. There were greater worlds beyond Sydney. I should seek them. But henceforth I should not make holiday for others by exposing my intentions.

As the train pulled in to Bowral, Moss Vale and each little station I pondered on the people who at first predicted that my head would be turned by flattery and lionisation, and a little later had accused me of being abnormal or petrified because no one had been able to make any impression on me except through my affections.

Well, there wasn't a woman among them who could hold a candle to Ma, not in housekeeping, in diction, in reading or in anything to which she addressed her talents. Ma could have kept a big institution shining and well-oiled in every wheel, and yet she was stuck in the bush in a situation in which her capabilities were as wasted as a cannon fired off to quell a mosquito—pure squanderation of the cannon and unnecessarily flattening to the skeet.

Thus I went from spoke to spoke till Goulburn, where I left the train and went to the Commercial for the remainder of the night.

211

CHAPTER TWENTY-ONE.

BACK ON THE LAND.

Eusty came to meet me with old Bandicoot and the
buggy. Mr. Blackshaw had come in with him to do a
little business and save horse-flesh. The day was a horror.
A western hurricane filled the world with wind gales, icy
as winter, and fogged the air with dust. There had been
no rain. There was no sign of spring.

I expected things to be rather desperate, remembering
what they had been a month ago, and letters from home
had had but one theme, but coming from the green coastal
belt, the city warmth, brightness and beauty, where people
daintily dressed rode on the comfortable trams and enjoyed
every other convenience and entertainment of existence,
the contrast was shocking. The bare cooked paddocks by
the way filled me with a feeling of despair.

"It's a good thing you didn't stay away any longer or
I reckon you would have had to walk home. Old Bandicoot is almost too poor to draw you," remarked Eusty,
giving the brave old friend an unnecessary flick of the
whip and raising the dust from his long shabby coat from
which his bones protruded.

Pa was about the same. "Serve him right," continued
Eusty. "He oughter learn not to be pokin' his nose so
close into the baits. We can take a short cut through
Burrawong, the gates ain't locked."

Burrawong was one of the larger stations in which much
of the good land of the district was locked. The cockies

212

usually had to follow the main road, but since the drought the owners had opened one of their permanent water-holes so that the poorer settlers could cart water to their homesteads. They were to be seen with a cask and a dray bucketing water into troughs to a few staggering animals which had been watered thus since January, now eight months past.

In a hot dust storm the sun shows as a ball of blood, this being a cold sirocco, it showed like a full moon. I shut my eyes against the whirling grit and wrapped my cape around me while Eusty urged poor old Bandicoot to keep toddling. In the paddocks of Burrawong, sheep skins lined the fences. The emaciated carcasses attracted flocks of black croakers and their dismal clamour filled the day.

"They've put on a couple of men to each paddock to skin the sheep as they die," remarked Mr. Blackshaw. "They'll have their work cut out after this wind. It topples the jumbucks over and they ain't got strength to get up again. There were a few clouds knocking about yestiddy, but this wind has cooked their chances. Burrawong is about cooked, and so are we."

"Like us," chimed Eusty. "Nearly all the cows pegged out while you were away. Old Roany and Nellie went first, and we have to lift up old Taralga twice a day; she can't hold out much longer."

A dray passed loaded with wood and drawn by three horses. The tears came as I noted the condition of the animals. That morning they had been lifted on to their feet, and yet they struggled so gallantly for their incompetent masters—panting, trembling, staggering through their purgatory under lash and objurgation. My heart seemed to suffocate.

Eusty's voice was crisp with cheerfulness. Drought and debt had no power to dispirit him—it took a stomach-ache or something personal. "What's making you so flaming down in the mug, Sybylla? It's us—who've been at home grafting away like fury while you were flying round among the toffs having a slashing time—that ought to hang our lip. Them city folks livin' on us people on the land!"

Bandicoot came to a dead stop opposite a man who was mending a gate. "Hello! The old moke still alive and kicking," he observed. "Might get rain next month," he continued hopefully. "Pet of a day ain't it?"

"We're about drove off of the land," said Mr. Blackshaw. "We'll have to join the unemployed and get seven bob a day minimum."

We dropped our passenger at the corner of his own fence and toiled on to our destination, Bandicoot's old coat sopping with the sweat of weakness.

"Put the poor old chap in the stable till he cools, and give him a handful of straw," commanded Pa.

Ma adjured us to get inside quickly and close the door. She had cleared the dust away twice that day, and was now going to desist until the wind subsided. Home was a dreary spectacle. Four-footed friends had died of their sufferings in my absence. Only the hardiest plants in the garden survived. Everything had a dirty grey film, irritating to the touch. Grit on the plates, grit between the teeth, grit on the pillow, grit in one's soul, ugh! An all-pervading smell of dust—ugh!

Dear old Pa was cheerful. He greeted me like a real friend and said we were better off than the people out West, whose homes were sometimes entirely buried in sand. He wanted to hear of everyone I had met, especially his former associates. When we were settled for the evening before the fire—one thing that the dust could not spoil—Pa, by eager questioning, had me telling of everyone I had met and what they said—with certain reservations.

"You saw Goring Hardy, did you have any talk with him?"

"Oh, yes, he was quite chatty, and advised me to go to London."

"How did he suggest finding the means?" inquired Ma.

"He dropped the suggestion when I told him how we are situated."   I did not add, and after he had found my maidenly citadel invulnerable.

"You've had a great holiday," interposed Aunt Jane. "Times have changed since I was a girl. If I had acted as you have, flouting modesty and blaspheming God, I should have been locked up on bread and water instead of being flattered and entertained. I don't know what the world is coming to with vulgarity and immorality."

"People will give you a little adulation, when it costs them nothing," remarked Ma with withering actuality, and got out the darning.

Bung went my Sydney career. I was back on the land at 'Possum Gully.

The dust storm took three days to clear away, and left everything in a deplorable condition.   It meant house-cleaning from end to end. I hated the coarse work after a taste of city luxury and conveniences, but I did not dare let my feelings escape me. The great adventure to Sydney had ended in débâcle. I sat amid the débris of hopes and expectations—only nebulous ones it is true, but all that I had had—and I had to grope my way out.

I produced the Lindsay drawings as a counter irritant. Ma dismissed them with one blast. She said that THAT was all that men cared for, but women soon had too much of it.

I left the book about just to see—well just to have the figures seen by Aunt Jane. Pa said that there was nothing immoral in the human body, that it was a work of NATURE. Aunt Jane agreed, but said that ******** **** * ***** ** God, but that delicacy should be maintained. She put on her specs and singled out an example. ***** *** Ma said Hhhh * *** ***** ******* ** ****** *****. I had not sufficient experience to refute such dicta. I hid the drawings at the bottom of a packing case.

No one mentioned Henry. He had not written to me lately, and was still away in Queensland. I hoped he had forgotten me, but should he have done so it would be one more nail in the coffin of AMOUR, another of Pan's "Half told Tales".*

So many kiss today, and die tomorrow:
And is remembrance sweet, or sweet and sorrow?
For some say only sweet; and sweet and bitter some . . .
Ah, who can end the tale, when all the dead are dumb!

As the days passed the mail brought a newspaper with Lady Jane's letter. She had a long paragraph about the departure of Mr. Goring Hardy, Australia's greatest literary man. He had been in demand among smart hostesses, and there would be an ache in more than one heart, Lady Jane dared suggest, when his ship carried him away from his native shores. No Australian girl had been able to interest him, but one beauty of the glorious eyes and velvety shoulders . . . Easy to discern this as Edmée. She was surely destined for a brilliant career matrimonially

* "Bulletin" Verse.
216

unless she was too ambitious and stayed too long in the stable, as Big Checks put it.

Lady Jane's letter kept me informed of those of her clients or victims whom I had met.

Aunt Jane asked me what I intended to do to help my parents. "You met Big Ears, why didn't you improve your chances there? And what about Mrs. Crasterton's brother?"

"I don't think anyone would want either of those," I murmured.

"Hadn't Mrs. Crasterton a son too?"

"Yes, but he's a terrible swell, wouldn't look at anything but a SOCIETY girl."

As the dreadful hot months dragged by, killing more and more suffering animals and pet plants and trees, I read that Big Ears had become engaged to a top notch SOCIETY girl who was also a tennis enthusiast. He was a valuable property as represented by Lady Jane. Glamour oozed from her tales of him. Yet I had discerned nought but a creature that I would have wilted to acknowledge as my mate. I hoped that Aunt Jane would miss the news of his wedding.

I found pluck to inquire of Pa what had happened to Old Grayling.

"Pillaloo!" grinned Pa. "He's kept in hobbles now. The flash buggy has disappeared." His daughters had come to see Pa and Ma specially to apologise for the old man's dementia. Silly old toad had made such a noise that it was one of the jokes of the district by now!

Horrors!

Our stoical land suffered, and we and the animals with it. The year ran down to harvest, a poor pinched harvest, but sufficient for the few remaining animals. I re-

217

ceived a cheque for my little book. The first instalment of three-pences had totted up to one hundred pounds. It was a lot of money to us. It saved us that year. There was also an editor on one of the big dailies who encouraged me to write prose sketches, and by these I sometimes made twenty-five shillings a week. He was gentle and kind and kept watch with his blue pencil against any originality that would have got me into trouble. At first I nearly sank through the boards because of the sentences he cut out—always those I had prized as my own discoveries. That they were deleted showed that I must be lacking in good form, but intuition quickly taught me what was acceptable.

I was able to write these articles at odd moments, and struggled more diligently with housewifery to offset the delinquency of attempting to write. An author enjoyed no prestige in 'Possum Gully.

My rebellious discontent surged up more furiously than ever. I craved the pang and tang, the joys and struggles of life at the flood. I was willing to accept my share of tears and pains if I could have also some of the splendour and passion which were my temperamental right. Was all my power of emotion wrong?—something to be suppressed till it evaporated like youth itself—something ladled out to me for a span and passed on to another futile creature of an hour?

On being honest with myself I felt that any God set up, except by little Mr. David, was contrary to a sane conception of a just and omnipotent God worth the name of Creator. The rubbish about self-will, and wrongs being righted in some foggy heaven could not stand against even little Jimmy Dripping common sense. The voice of the wind urges the soul to deeper conceptions of spiritual wisdom. The magic in the wide sunlight cancels the trivial church image of a God fashioned on the pattern of an unprepossessing old man. The contentment preached by pastors and masters to the less fortunate in goods and opportunities sounds like an impudent assumption of betterism by those who are often in the worse collection of parasites. Why should Ma's extraordinary skill and management, which enables her to excel a fashionable *couturière* and equal a *chef* and baker, be wasted, while poor old Lady Hobnob—to take one example—who cannot overcome B FLATS has a glorious mansion in a heavenly situation at Potts Point? Why should Pa, who had tried to help the struggling men by fearless and honest measures, have been robbed of his property while a vulgar old vulture like Sir James Hobnob, who had diverted to himself a fortune out of public funds, should have all the honours and be invited by the King to dine at Buckingham Palace and to sleep at Windsor Castle? I hated all the doctrines of 'Possum Gully and its want of works, but had given up saying so aloud.

About Easter there was a bobbery in Lady Jane's column. What do you guess? A SOCIETY WEDDING. A BEAUTY and a CONFIRMED BACHELOR. Most notable wedding of the year. OLD FAMILIES, SOCIETY, all were marshalled. Shower bouquets, a dozen bridesmaids—a big galanty show.

I laughed to picture Gaddy in the middle of bridal flutter. What would he do with his corporation—ah, what . . .

No; I did not envy Edmée her bridegroom. Quite the reverse. Nevertheless, I did seem a petty failure with my hands showing more glaringly than ever the effects of coarse manual toil, and my feet still unacquainted with silk stockings, while there was Edmée in satin and orange blossoms filling the newspapers with her success. I envied her her suitability to success, her disregard of consistency, her obliviousness of personal detractors.

I could not complain of lack of opportunities. I wondered how many other women Goring Hardy had practically kidnapped for a week just for their company and nothing but kisses—ardent but respectable? Yet I had not improved the shining hour.

I had fled from Gaddy in such a way that he had protected his vanity by pretending that his advances were spoof. In Big Ears, the catch of the previous season, I had discerned only a flap-eared weakling who stuttered prayers. He had offered to abrogate prayers until I was "saved", but no, here I was back in 'Possum Gully and he not yet returned from a tour in Spain, and I had nought but a dream tho' it ne'er came true.

Bung! Bung! Pop! Pop! went all respect for romance. Edmée could put Gaddy in the position of the romantic lover and affinity that she had gushed about. Gaddy, who had scoffed at Edmée, succumbed to her. Big Ears, who was going to commit suicide for love of me, forgot in a day. Marriage evidently was a piece of trading: one took the best animal procurable and got on with it. Ah, me! Oh, well!

I wrote things at odd times, things that I wanted to write, different from those I wrote to please the kind Editor, who was desirous of helping me with bread and butter. But nothing found favour with publishers or editors in Sydney or Melbourne. They said they expected something *different* from me. I gave thought to this, based upon their suggestions for acceptability. I deduced that I *was* different, and that they wanted me to be the same as all the others, to be one of the reigning school. Also they had stories from England. Their readers preferred English stories.

Well, so did I. I had had no notions about realistic Australianism until misdirected by old Harris. He had brought upon me all this trouble, this defeat. I wrote to ask him whither now?

I never had a reply. He was dead.

Any poor LOCAL CACKLERS who wrote to me and of which, with my OWN HOOK conceit, I was emphatically one, were assured that there was no hope for anyone in Australia. We must by hook or harpoon get away to THE BIG SMOKE.

For what does it matter if a scribe gain the encouragement of CRITICS and become the hope of the booksellers and circulating libraries that he will write a second bestseller, if the scribe himself does not gain enough profit either to earn the respect of those he lives among or to escape from them?

It was not that I did not hanker for the fleshpots of life, but that I was not constituted to accept the conditions which went with those offered to me. This depressed me acutely, for I was of a sociable nature and loved all that radiance and beauty of the world and life which is open only to those with means.

I had managed to alleviate my early unhappiness about God by discrediting the unpleasant representations of His vindictiveness with which religions abound, by crediting only what was beautiful and noble in conception and by eschewing prayer as a superstition. This helped to diminish God the tyrant, but I had not found God the refuge and helper. One of my elderly friends-by-correspondence was warning me against self-pity as a debilitating

221

affliction and directing my mind towards philosophy, but philosophy is rather an arid diet when one is hungry for adventure and romance.

Thus went the days with empty heads and dusty feet.

'Possum Gully fell back to normal after throwing me up. It grew poorer socially. The genial and conversable Father O'Toole was succeeded by a man with beetling brows and a brogue to match. Our R.C. friends invited us to his inauguration, at which he berated his flock and ordered them to have nothing to do with Protestants under penalty of purgatory. The Reverend peasant was doubtless ambitious for a bishopric, for it seems that in creeds or politics the less Christianity and reason and the more partisanship the surer the official rewards and honours for the protagonists.

Dear little Mr. David had likewise departed. In his stead we had a visitation of English curates. Eusty said they talked like choking magpies, and many a time he had to be driven from the entertainment of mimicking them to his work. They seldom called. They preferred the richer fleshpots of Burrawong, venerated the owner as a "squiah" and mistakenly relegated all cockies to those who should order themselves lowly and reverently to their "bettahs".

Billy Olliver had removed to a place near Inverell. From the day of the Show I had not seen him nor heard from him. Henry's consequence had evidently scared him from the course. Billy's friend, the teacher who had come in Old Harris's place, took me to task over Billy. He said it was a cruel thing to have broken Billy's heart—such a true honest fellow—no frill about him, but a thorough gentleman. How could I break his heart when he had never opened the question of love with me at all, how did

222

Billy's spokesman know that it was not my heart that had been trifled with? EXPERIENCE was showing me that this breaking of hearts and the hope of constancy in AMOUR were mirages like those encountered in the delirium of typhoid fever. I had to take refuge in dreams—dreams of the distant fields so green because they were far away.

Chapter Twenty-Two.

So to Speak!

Henry Beauchamp was nearly a year away in Queensland. The seasons there enabled him to take up the slack of his property pinched by drought in the Southern District. He came back overland, arriving first at Moongudgeonby, or Five-Bob Downs, as it had come to be known, as he said, over his head and under his nose, because of my pranks.

The warnings against his fickleness were contradicted by his actions, but the smut of certain allegations remained like the smoke from a railway engine when you get in a tunnel. Renewed business around Goulburn enabled him to spend a lot of time at 'Possum Gully.

We reopened our old battles, he being armoured in the dogma that it was NATURE for women to serve men and bring children into the world regardless of whether or not the world was a fit place to receive them. He said he could give me much more than I could ever make by writing. "Marriage," he insisted, "gives a woman standing. If she gets hold of a fellow with any sort of a head on him she has lots more standing than sour old school teachers and these other old maids, on their own, can have."

STANDING!

"You don't allow a woman any standing at all except by being the annexation of a man," I said.

He laughed in his large healthy way. "Well, I did not arrange the world."

"Yes, but you could help rearrange it," I flashed, though

224

I knew that among all the billions of men in the world there were few so just and brave that they would attempt any rearrangement that would lessen their top-dog self-confidence and loot; and none of these except Pa had ever undergone a sojourn at 'Possum Gully.

"You'll have the vote when you are old enough. The rearranging of the world is in your own hands now; and I voted for woman suffrage."

"There's a lot of evolution in that, and evolution like posterity will be rather late in doing anything for the current generation."

"Oh, Lord, I can't make out how you can have so much rebellion in such a small soft frame."

Many less stupid men than he would be surprised if they could see into the hearts of women who lie beside them so passively, or could hear what they say when the ogres of their bosom cannot hear.

"You'll find women more against your ideas than men."

"That is because they think it will please men—merely a matter of business advertisement."

"Ah," he continued complacently. "You are not meant to be one of those brainy old man-haters who would rather have a snake around than a child. You were meant for love and motherhood."

"Man-haters," I contended, "are those who are game enough to object to the present state of affairs for their motherhood. One such woman has more power of deep loving than half-a-dozen of the namby-pamby over-sexed womanised things "

"Look here," I warn Henry over and over again, "don't you risk me in the matrimonial basket. Throw your handkerchief on one of the dozens of girls and widows who would snatch it eagerly. The world is infested with women

225

who will agree with you—little darlings without intelligence, and boastful of it, who have been trained to be afraid of the night and to screech at a mouse and all that sort of thing. I love being out alone in the night, and mice could sleep in my pocket without frightening me."

If we are out riding when these discussions take place, he chews a few more gum leaves and says, "Thank you, no. The dolls have no spirit. I'd sooner marry a cow. I'd run away from a doll in three weeks."

He has the same mentality as Goring Hardy—take the world as it is and be comfortable and a success. Take me and set to work to squash me into the groove of the noodles.. The difference between Mr. Hardy and Mr. Beauchamp is in their interests, Henry's being those of a man on the land and the politics appertaining thereto, and Goring having the literary tastes and politics of the Londoner.

"After your first child," Henry maintains, "you'll settle down as steady as a church."

My first child! Something to break my spirit and tether me to the domestic tread-mill! Had he known my dreams of a first child he would not have uttered that mistake.

Even so, a first child need not last for ever. It could contribute to the fulfilment of life if it were not followed by a dozen others. I claim the same right as all the Father O'Toole's to be a spiritual parent of my race rather than to submit to the ideal or to follow the example of the mother rabbit.

I repudiate the crawl theory that we should be servile to our parents or to God for the bare fact of a mean existence. Most people are satisfied with a world run in a wasteful insanitary fashion. I am not. They are unashamed that seventy-five per cent. of human beings are

226

fit only for the scrap heap. I am not. They are thankful to thrive while others starve. I am not.

I rebel with all my lung force against sitting down under life as it is, and as for a first child being an instrument of enslavement, both for his own and his mother's sake, 'twere better he should never be.

The two greatest women in Australia are unmarried, and it would be a good plan for a few more to support them, to remain free to ventilate the state of marriage and motherhood and to reform its conditions.

"You just talk through your hat to be entertaining," Henry continued after a while. "You'll have to marry someone."

"Why?"

"You could not endure to be despised as an old maid who could not get a man."

At that I galloped right away from him leaving him a far speck on the glistening road that rises towards Lake George. I galloped until Popinjay was blown. Henry would not overtax Black-Dappled Grey to carry his sixteen stone at top speed. I reined-in on the crest from which far to the south can be seen the dreaming peaks of the mountains beyond the Murrumbidgee. Their beauty is a banner of spiritual strength raised for me to follow away from 'Possum Gully limitations.

Never in face of that wide brilliance of eternity stretched on space would I give in to mental decay and a dun dim routine calling for nothing beyond the endowment of a halfwit.

Despised for being an old maid, indeed! Why are men so disturbed by a woman who escapes their spoliation? Is her refusal to capitulate unendurable to masculine egotism, or is it a symptom of something more fundamental?

Why have men invented monogamy? All the laws, all the philosophies and religions of academic education, as well as organised fighting and politics, are men's inventions and are preserved by men as their special concern and business.

I chuckled into Popinjay's twitching ears to imagine the shock my ideas in this direction would be for grandmas of the tame hen order and for Celibate Fathers. Of all the people I knew perhaps only two or three would discuss my theories without hysteria, though bishops and great-aunts can accept harlots as necessary and count technical virgins as more worthy of honour. This was another thought which to utter would be madness, and which to suppress seems canting cowardice.

Henry came jogging up with his strong white teeth showing in a smile. "What thought smote you to run away like that?" he demanded.

I diverted him with a bit of surface smartness. "I was thinking that it must be difficult to sustain the fragrance and escape the frowsiness of marriage: singleness would be more aesthetic."

"Is that all! Now tell me if you could order a man to fit your ideas, what would he be like?"

I did not reply that it would be one who could put his finger on some hidden spring in himself and in me and in grand fusion reveal the fullness of life.

"Come now, what's this fellow to be like?"

"At least he would not be afraid of freedom and the light of understanding for women as well as men. His mind would not prescribe asinine limitations for women as part of God's will. He would not take rabies at the idea of a world where there would be no hungry children, no unprovided old age, and he would be ashamed to have harlots at street corners awaiting his patronage and then come to clean girls and blither about LOVE."

"Hooray! Tell me some more."

"There are other things he wouldn't be that I have learned from old wives' gossip, but I cannot enumerate them without being indecent. So many old wives take all the sweetness out of life because life has taken all the joy and sweetness out of them: and lastly, no potting, panning and puddening for me for a set of noodles that might as well remain unborn for all that they attain."

When Henry next caught up to me he said, "You have two years more to get these notions off your chest. They are no end of fun."

He refuses to release me until the 39-21 hour has arrived. As he will then be within a month of 40, and refuses to wait any longer because 39 will look so much better on the marriage certificate. I have not quite dismissed him because only in marriage can respectable women satisfy curiosity. The penalties for violating the social code are so painful that they are avoided by the sensitive with the care exercised against smashing over a precipice. Thrice free must be the innate wantons or the coarse who can plumb all heights and depths of curiosity and suck entertainment where they list unhampered by the agony of shame. The over-sensitive risk many chances of atrophying by the wayside.

Popinjay was restive for her foal, shut up at home, and grew so fractious that I had to relinquish argument and give myself fully to the delight of handling her as she reefed and plunged. At length I gave her her head at full gallop down the long steep incline, feeling sure that she could keep on her feet and I in my saddle on her round slippery back.

229

CHAPTER TWENTY-THREE.

THERE IS ENGLAND.

My dear Editor has gone away out of the Colony—or
State as we call it since Federation. Perhaps he grew
tired of taking himself out of himself as well as myself
out of me to find acceptance. He has gone to a different
kind of paper, and I am left without a patron. It must be
grand to be free to write what you like, happier still
to be so self-satisfied as to like what you write.

One amelioration is mine. I have lately received from
the stately publishing house of McMurwood a letter in
character. It is now time for my book to go into a final
form and become a CLASSIC. Surprise number 1: as I
thought only Vergil, Homer, Aristophanes and Co. were
CLASSICS and that to couple the word with a LOCAL
CACKLER would be blasphemy or caricature. Surprise
number 2: that I could have any say in a re-issue. Could
the book be stopped altogether? Through imaginary
characters being identified with real people I was accused
of belittling my connections, but if no more books were
forthcoming those in circulation would die of old age and
disappear and we could all sink to peace. In future I
could have a *nom de plume,* carefully guarded, so that my
attempts could be taken on their own demerits without the
impetus of scandal. Conventional people and I would not
then suffer from a relationship uncongenial to both parties
and for which neither is responsible.

Messrs. McMurwood met my wishes as if I were a

real person—an experience to give me back a shred of self-confidence. Honesty and decency are basic necessities, but good manners are to the sensibilities as cream and honey to the tongue. Certainly I can withdraw the book. Would I care for a number of the remaining copies for my own use? No, not one. And that was that. If only I had known this after the first edition: but a number of LOCAL CACKLERS had given me the benefit of their EXPERIENCE with MSS bought and published on Australia's own publishing hook. They had been given ten or twenty pounds, and though the works in some instances sold as well or better than mine, the authors were not entitled to nor did they receive a penny beyond the first amount, nor were they allowed any control even in revising subsequent editions. There was a case where learning by another's EXPERIENCE resulted in knowledge as limiting as ignorance.

I am now twenty. The years have passed droughtily in a personal as well as a meteorological sense. I feel so terribly old. I have dried up in this barren gully while there are such glorious places elsewhere. If only I had a view of mountains or of the sea in storm, or in sun too calm for waves but glinting like the silver gum leaves in the noonday light, this would be to know wealth despite money poverty.

Only the trouble with God has abated. LIFE and LOVE and WORK insist increasingly. The need to submit to marriage or else find some other way of earning my living grows nearer, clearer, deadlier than before. Fortunately Henry Beauchamp has had to go to Queensland again to look after his property. It is a safe distance offering respite for the present.

231

The idea of marriage is going bung with me. Marriage is unnecessarily engulfing and too full of opportunities to experience GREY TOPPER'S receipt for producing genius.

Henry once said that he would be jealous of my writing if it took up my spare time when he needed me. In short, my brain-children would be proscribed. I am weary of Henry's indulgent but inflexible assumption that my ideas are mere vivacity or girlish coquetry, which motherhood will extirpate. I can discern under the padded glove of spooniness the fixed determination to bend me to prescribed femaleness. Ah, no, m'lord, the bait is not sufficiently enticing, nor does it entirely conceal the hook.

I have refuged in day-dreams, but one must have more than these on which to expend emotion: there must be some object of passion, personal or public. Mine is the beauty of the universe. And there is always England. England with her ancient historic beauty—tradition—the racial rooftree. I picture her cool green fields, her misty downs, her bare woods under the snow, her young leaves and soft flowers in spring. Her castles and cathedrals, her ivied towers, her brooks are as clear to my nostrils and closed eyes as the scents and features of 'Possum Gully. And there is London with its romantic fogs, its crowds and ceremonial pageants, Rotten Row and the Mall, the British Museum, the Mansion House, The Tower and Westminster. I know London much better than I do Sydney. Through song and story it has permeated every fibre of my mind since I could first scan a pictured page, while I have spent scarcely a month in but one corner of Sydney. London—THE BIG SMOKE—London, where our dreams come true.

232

England acclaimed my first homespun effort. England may welcome my second and third. I will arise and go to Mother England.

Lady Jane's column is devoted to escapees. Sculptors, writers, singers, actors, painters, educationists, politicians all depart inevitably. I have been going with them in imagination ever since I saw the Heads standing up there with the spray playing around their base and the Pacific beyond like a high blue plateau. It seems that only those remain who cannot get away, those who are tied to pots and pans by poverty and ignorance, by misfortune or incompetence.

The seasons have smiled once more. The chief reminder of the drought which killed the stock and bared the paddocks is that here and there a spot of richer green shows where in death some animal fertilised its pasture. The doubled value of remaining stock compensates for what was lost. Ridge and gully echo the cry of young things which replenish the earth.

The day is lovely in the atmosphere and ample draperies of November. Even 'Possum Gully, like a plain girl when happy, has a meed of beauty. The afternoon is hot and clear as though the sun were a box-wood fire. The flowers droop their heads in the fierce proud heat, lizards bask in the glare, the poultry spread their wings and pant in the shade, the cows lie in the reeds of the waterhole on the flat, the horses stand head to tail in pairs under the quince hedge rising above the orchard fence and stamp and switch the flies off themselves.

A tiny breeze goes flirting through the last of afternoon, the eschscholtzias furl their silken petals. I have ascended the hill behind which the sun departs and where a thousand times I have watched him gleam red as a fire between the trunks of the grey messmates and powdered brittle-gums. To the east, amid wild hop scrub and stringy-barks, a bridle track threads its way to the crisp main road to Goulburn, and on and on to Sydney, where the sea tracks lead on to the WORLD.

The final gleam of the sun kisses the waterhole, the shadows grow long and dark, reversing their morning journey. The rumble of a train miles distant bears my heart on its rhythm of departure. The kookaburras are laughing themselves to sleep, chorus answering chorus— *coda—da capo—finale*. The gentle curlews lure me farther into the scrub, where I still can see the departing sun and the afterglow falling far away through a gap in the ranges on to one of the bright rich plains of an early holding.

The flaunting afterglow melts and passes, the evening star is bright and bold, and throws a spark in the dam of the back paddock at the fall of the she-oak ridge where the night birds call in unmolested scrubs and flap slowly from tree to tree. A tremor of night runs along the seeding grasses.

A wise old moon slowly chases the shadows westward once again and laps all in her silver enchantment. A thousand jewels flash above the dark shadows as she catches the eyes of the flock camped on the rise.

Beauty is abroad. Under her spell the voices of the great world call me. To them I give ear and go.